You're invited to a

CREEPOVER™

Is She for Real?

written by P. J. Night

SIMON SPOTLIGHT
New York London Toronto Sydney New Delhi

SIMON SPOTLIGHT
An imprint of Simon & Schuster Children's Publishing Division
1230 Avenue of the Americas, New York, New York 10020

Text by Kama Einhorn
Designed by Nicholas Sciacca
For information about special discounts for bulk purchases, please contact Simon & Schuster Special Sales at 1-866-506-1949 or business@simonandschuster.com.
Manufactured in the United States of America 0312 OFF
First Edition 10 9 8 7 6 5 4 3 2 1
ISBN 978-1-4424-5056-1
ISBN 978-1-4424-5057-8 (eBook)
Library of Congress Catalog Card Number 2012930111

PROLOGUE

A figure walked through the fog onto the sand. It was dark and visibility was poor, except for the thin beam of light shining on the ocean from the full moon above.

He crossed the beach, his fine leather shoes covered in sand up to the silver buckles, but he paid that no mind.

The man wore a thick woolen cloak. He stood in the dark in front of the roaring waves and spoke softly.

"I am sorry for all the days I spent at sea, my lady. I am sorry for every day that I did not spend with you."

His voice grew louder, and he dug his hand into the pocket of his waistcoat to clutch the ring.

"I have burned all your things, milady, having kept only this ring to remember you by. This ring that I slipped on your finger because I loved you so. But you were never the same after that."

He paused, now overtaken by sobs.

Please believe me, he thought.

After a moment, he gathered himself and held the ring above his head.

"This ring . . . this ring is to blame . . . *I curse this ring!*"

He hurled it into the sea.

CHAPTER 1

Nate Carlson was psyched to take his metal detector to the beach. The walk to the beach was a short one because the beach was right behind his house. "The beach is my backyard!" Nate used to tell his friends when he was little. He supposed he got that line from his parents, who said it all the time. It was true, anyway, and pretty awesome. There was a small lawn between his house and the beach, but that was it. Nate felt that wonderful familiar feeling of anticipation as he approached the sand. It was a cloudy, windy day, so he had the beach to himself.

Slipping off his shoes, Nate stepped onto the cool sand. He switched on the metal detector and started walking, scanning the sand back and forth.

A large black bird swooped near his head. As he ducked,

he thought of his twin sister, Lissa. That bird would have sent her running home. Birds totally creeped her out, especially when they flapped too close to her head. He looked up to see a few of them circling above. The others were dive-bombing the water, catching food. They would drop straight down out of the sky, beak forward, disappear into the water, then come up with a crab struggling in their beaks.

It was cool to watch. He had never noticed this type of bird before, but then again, he never paid much attention to birds.

Beep, beep, beep! Nate's thoughts about birds were interrupted by the sound of the metal detector going off. Nate bent down and dug around a little. All he found was an old, crushed tin can. He left it there and kept walking, looking at the variety of shells along the tide line. His favorite were the jackknife clams, which were long and thin, and the jingle shells, which his mother called "angels' toenails" because of their golden shiny hue. Nate's mom said a lot of things that, in Nate's opinion, were pretty corny.

Beep, beep, beep! He dropped to his knees and dug around, not finding anything at all. But when he scanned the spot again, the detector kept beeping. He dug deeper—still nothing. But when he scanned the spot again, *beep, beep, beep!*

He dug deeper than he had before, the sand growing colder and damper the deeper he went. He felt around in the sand for something, anything, but couldn't find the source of what was setting off the detector. But still . . . *Beep, beep, beep!*

He had dug maybe three feet down with his bare hands when a tiny flash of gold caught his eye. He fished around until his fingers closed around something. Pulling his hand free, Nate looked in his palm and saw it: A small, perfect ruby ring. *This may actually be treasure,* Nate thought. He sat and stared at it as he brushed the sand off with the bottom of his shirt, squinting to get a better look. He realized that the late afternoon sun had gone down, and the sky had suddenly grown quite dark. A strange feeling settled over him just then. He looked around—had anyone seen him find this ring? Should he show someone? The strange feeling grew deeper, and on some level, Nate realized he felt very nervous all of a sudden. Were there rules of buried treasure? Should he call the police?

What is going on with me? Nate wondered, trying to

dismiss the feeling and focus, instead, on his discovery. But before he could do either, a loud *crack* startled him. He looked up to see a brilliant flash of lightning over the ocean. *I'd better get home fast,* Nate thought. He had promised his parents he'd never use the metal detector outside on the beach in stormy weather. The sun had been shining just a few moments ago, but a storm was definitely coming. Nate knew it wasn't safe to be outside with the metal detector during a lightning storm. Quickly shoving the ring deep in his pocket, he ran to gather his shoes and head inside.

I am the owner of actual buried treasure, he thought as he walked, the ring safely in his pocket. *But what do I do with it? Maybe I should give it to my love.* He almost laughed out loud at the thought. *Ha! There are no girls at school I even like that way, much less love.*

When Nate got home, he deposited his metal detector on the enclosed porch in the back of the house and headed inside for a snack. Standing in the kitchen at the side of the house, he saw a moving van parked on his street. Three men were carrying boxes and furniture into the empty house on the other side of the graveyard. If Nate's backyard was the beach, his "side yard" was a graveyard, which was just as unique, but not quite as much fun, since his parents didn't exactly let him hang out there. At the other side of the graveyard was a large house that had been vacant for months, since old Mr. Reiney had passed away. But it looked like someone was finally moving in. Nate was curious and headed back out the door to investigate.

Crossing the graveyard, he saw a couple about his parents' age, an older woman, and a girl about his age standing on the porch of the house. As he approached, the couple waved and the girl smiled.

Nate wasn't shy. He waved back and smiled at the girl.

The man was the first to speak. "Hello there!" he called. "Come on up to the porch!" He and his wife and the old lady and the girl were all looking at Nate.

The girl was beautiful, with long, curly blond hair that swooped over one eye, and the lightest, brightest blue eyes Nate had ever seen.

"I'm Richard, and this is my wife, Sally, and my aunt Mimi," he said, gesturing toward the old woman, who smiled but didn't say anything. "And this is our daughter, Bethany."

Bethany smiled at Nate. "Hi," she said simply. Nate

stood and stared at Bethany, trying to think of something to say. His mind was suddenly blank.

Think, Nate! Speak! Say something! "Hi," he finally said to the small group. "I'm Nate Carlson, and I live over there on the other side of the graveyard. My parents run the bed-and-breakfast, but we live there too." He pointed to his house. "I guess the neighbors in between our houses can't really introduce themselves," he added, then cringed at his attempt at humor. *Did that sound lame?* he wondered.

But Bethany laughed, so Nate relaxed.

"Well, it's nice to meet you, Nate," Richard said. "You two look about the same age. Are you in seventh grade?"

"Yes." Nate nodded.

"Well, I guess we'll be seeing each other in school then," Bethany said. She gave a quick wave and went into the house.

"Well, bye," Nate said to the group.

"Great meeting you, Nate," Bethany's mom said.

"You too. See you later." Nate turned and headed home, all the time forcing himself not to turn around to see if Bethany had come back out of the house.

CHAPTER 2

Early the next morning on her way downstairs to breakfast, Lissa Carlson rolled her eyes as she sprang down the steps and passed the familiar framed story that hung in the entryway:

Welcome to the Warwick Inn!

In 1659 Lord and Lady Warwick arrived from England to establish a new settlement in Connecticut. Because they were the leaders of the original group of settlers, the town was named for them.

Lady Warwick was a legendary beauty, with pale skin, emerald-green eyes, and ruby-red lips. It is said that she always wore her long black hair poker straight and parted precisely in the middle, though that style was not at all in vogue during her lifetime. During the last few years of her young life, she always wore a ruby ring that had been a gift from her beloved husband. Legend has it that Lord Warwick brought the ring to her as a peace offering after returning from a long fishing voyage.

Lord Warwick loved the sea and would often go on very long fishing voyages. While he was away, Lady Warwick worried constantly about his safety, but she was also very jealous and became convinced he had a mistress. Lord Warwick returned from what was to be his final voyage to find Lady Warwick very ill. She was also very angry and claimed he had broken her heart by being untrue to her. Soon after, she fell into a coma and died, and the bereaved Lord Warwick buried her behind their home.

Years later, when Lord Warwick (who had since become the town's governor) moved to a different house nearby, he had her coffin dug up to be moved to the land of his new house. The grave diggers found the coffin suspiciously light, so they opened it up. They found the inside of the coffin scratched up . . . and Lady Warwick's body GONE! Lord Warwick and her doctor had buried her alive. Presumably they had been unable to detect a faint heartbeat without a stethoscope. But where was her body?

To avoid suspicion of witchcraft, Lord Warwick had the coffin burned and ordered all her possessions burned as well. He lived out the rest of his days alone, and left the instruction that upon his death, he was to be buried in the town graveyard, with Lady Warwick's gravestone placed next to his.

Local legend says that if you hear the wind tapping at your window in the town of Old Warwick, it's really Lady Warwick's ghost trying to get back inside to reunite with her beloved husband. And she's still brokenhearted and angry, so watch out!

Bouncing into the kitchen, Lissa found her parents sipping coffee at the breakfast table. She grabbed a waffle off the plate. Nate was already halfway through his waffle, which he had slathered in his usual combination of peanut butter and bananas, with honey drizzled on top. His shaggy hair half obscured his face. Lissa preferred her waffles with just a touch of peanut butter and a pat of jelly.

Lissa and Nate were twins, and their faces certainly looked similar, but their personal styles couldn't have been more different. Nate had a disheveled skateboarder look, while Lissa kept herself very tidy and wore her hair short. They both had dark blond hair and big brown eyes, and the same exact dimples when they smiled.

"These are very strange children," said Mrs. Carlson, addressing her husband. "They seem to think their waffles are slices of bread and it's lunchtime. Who doesn't want butter and syrup on a waffle?"

"Go figure," said Mr. Carlson, smiling at Nate and Lissa as they happily munched their waffles. They had to eat quickly to get the bus in time. As they ate, their parents discussed the B and B business of the day: which guests were coming, which were checking out, and other fascinating matters.

"I'm going to try making a new granola this week," said Mrs. Carlson. "It's going to have cranberries and cashews."

"Sounds amazing," Mr. Carlson said. "I did love last week's, though, with the dried blueberries and the coconut. What about the scones? Do we have any more dried cherries for the cherry-ginger version you made a while ago? That was a big hit."

"We have the cherries, but I only have fresh ginger, and that recipe called for sweetened, crystallized ginger," Mrs. Carlson said. "But I'll go online and figure out how to crystallize it myself. It can't be too hard."

"Excellent," Mr. Carlson said, smiling happily at his wife.

"Hey, everyone, did you notice the moving truck at the house on the other side of the graveyard yesterday?" Mrs. Carlson asked.

"Oh yeah," Nate said, trying to sound like it was no big deal. Like the truck hadn't contained the possessions of the most beautiful girl he'd ever laid eyes on. "I meant to tell you. A family moved in there. They're nice." He tried to make it sound as simple as possible: *They're nice.*

"Really?" Lissa said. "Are there kids?"

"Uh, yeah, one," Nate replied. "A girl. And she's in seventh grade, so I'm sure we'll be seeing her in school." *I hope I see her at school,* he added silently.

"Yay!" Lissa said. "Finally a kid in the neighborhood! What's she like?"

"I dunno. She's cool," Nate said, and stuffed his face with waffle to avoid talking any more about Bethany.

"Well, I'm glad someone's finally moving in," Mr. Carlson said. "That's a great house, and I'm excited to meet our new neighbors. The neighborhood hasn't felt the same since Mr. Reiney passed away." Elderly Mr. Reiney had lived alone in that house and had been the president of the Old Warwick Historical Society.

"I know. Maybe they'll join the historical society," Mrs. Carlson said hopefully.

Nate and Lissa met each other's glance, and Nate rolled his eyes the exact same way Lissa did. Their parents were an endless source of entertainment for them.

But the truth was, their parents loved their jobs owning and operating the Warwick Inn. The family lived in a wing that was mostly separate from the main part of the B and B, so it wasn't too weird, and sometimes Nate and Lissa would go for days without seeing a single guest.

Tourists came from all over to get a dose of town history, which Lissa's parents were more than happy to give them. The walls of the inn were full of historical photos, documents, and maps, including the ghost story above the staircase. Apparently, to some people, the history of colonial Connecticut was all the rage. Who were these people? Nate and Lissa often wondered.

"Remember, you said Olivia and Lily could sleep over Friday night," Lissa reminded her mom. "We're going to make cookie dough and then not bake it. Just eat it."

"Right, Liss," her mom said. "That's fine, of course you can have your sleepover. But I wish you wouldn't eat raw dough. It'll make you sick."

"I disagree," Nate said thoughtfully, rubbing his chin, as if commenting on something of great importance. "I've eaten plenty of raw cookie dough in my time, without incident."

"Oh, have you, young sir?" his dad said with a laugh. "Hurry up, the two of you, before you miss the bus."

Lissa grabbed her backpack and turned to her mother. "That's what kids do at sleepover parties," she said. "It's not like we sit around and tell ghost stories."

"Well, I don't see why not," her mom replied earnestly. "You've got the best ghost story in the country right here in this town. But suit yourself!" Lissa smiled and rolled her eyes one more time as she and Nate took off.

The bus stopped right next door to the Carlsons', in front of the old graveyard, where Lord Warwick was buried next to the gravestone of Lady Warwick. This had been a huge selling point twenty years ago, when the Carlsons were looking for a property to start their B and B.

Another big selling point was that the site of Lord and Lady Warwick's original home, the home she died in and had been buried next to, was just a few blocks away. There was no actual house there because Lord Warwick had it burned to the ground after she died. There was just a historical marker on a large stone.

These days, the B and B's website indicated the location of the graveyard and included a cheesy warning to prospective guests: "Come to Old Warwick and meet new friends at the Warwick Inn. Who knows . . . maybe you'll even meet the ghost of Lady Warwick!"

Nate and Lissa had an old, ongoing joke with their parents about that sentence. They'd repeat it to fit whatever situation they were faced with. If Lissa had a cold, for instance, Nate would say, "Come to Old Warwick and meet new friends at the Warwick Inn. Who knows . . . maybe you'll even meet a stuffy-nosed, cranky kid!"

Or, when their parents were hanging wallpaper to perfectly match the original Yankee kitchen style, Lissa would say, "Who knows . . . maybe you'll even meet two obsessive amateur historians!"

But the website must have said something right because the Warwick Inn was awfully popular. The NO VACANCY sign was constantly up in front of the house, and guests really seemed to enjoy themselves. Nate and Lissa's parents always made guests feel at home, with special touches like homemade cookies in their room upon arrival.

They were also happy to give full tours of the place and explain exactly how each part of the house had been restored. They'd even pull books off the shelf about the town history and show the guests how homes looked way back when, and how the inn matched the descriptions. And they'd walk with them through the overgrown-with-weeds graveyard to show them Lord and Lady Warwick's gravestones, which were kind of hard to find if you didn't know where they were.

Corny as she thought the whole legend of Lady Warwick was, Lissa mostly avoided the cemetery. The few times she'd entered the graveyard, she felt totally creeped out. Something about Lord and Lady Warwick's gravestones made her feel really nervous and scared. But she'd never admitted that to Nate. She knew he would never let her live it down.

CHAPTER 3

As they stepped off the bus, Lissa saw Olivia's purple backpack right away. Practically everything Olivia owned was purple. It was an interesting look, given Olivia's bright red hair.

They waved to each other and walked to their lockers. Nate was already off with his friends, and the girls still had some time before homeroom, which they had with their friend Lily. Nate was in a different homeroom. The school separated twins as much as possible as a matter of policy, though Lissa wouldn't have minded having classes with Nate. She was pretty much used to being side by side with him in every other way.

"We're on for Friday night," Lissa reminded Olivia. "Sleepover. My house. Cookie dough. Totally raw."

Olivia smiled to reveal the purple rubber bands around the tiny metal squares of her braces. "Excellent," she said. "Lily is psyched too."

"And my mom is obsessed with her new scone recipes," Lissa added. "Who knows, maybe we'll even eat something that's cooked." They spun the locks to their lockers and opened them, putting books in and taking books out. The inside of Olivia's locker was full of purple stickers and ribbons, plus photos of her, Olivia, and Lily doing fun stuff together: burying one another in sand at the beach, dressed up on Halloween, on the Ferris wheel at the town fair, and on a class trip to New York City, atop the Empire State Building. Lissa had some of the very same photos inside her own locker.

As they walked to homeroom, Lissa thought about what a great year it had been with her friends. She'd never been part of a gang of three before, and she loved it. That old phrase "two's company, three's a crowd" never seemed to apply to them. Instead they were like a chemistry experiment in which all three chemicals reacted perfectly with one another to create some bubbling, colorful potion.

The homeroom routine was always the same. The kids

sat in a circle with their homeroom teacher, Ms. Lang, who asked them how things were going, what was happening in their classes, what issues were coming up with schoolwork and friends, and so on. If there were problems, the group tried to come up with solutions. When they got to the circle, only Ms. Lang and a new girl were sitting there.

"Hi, girls," Ms. Lang said to Lissa and Olivia. Just then Lily entered, her straight black hair halfway down her back. They all sat down, along with a few other kids who had entered the room at the same time.

"Everyone, we have a new student in our school today," Ms. Lang said, gesturing toward the girl next to her, who had long, curly blond hair. "This is Bethany Warren, and she's just moved here from New York City. Welcome, Bethany. Let's all introduce ourselves and offer one thing we can do to help her first day go smoothly."

Bethany seemed totally relaxed, and not at all nervous to be meeting a room full of kids for the first time. She smiled and made eye contact with each of the other students.

"Lily, why don't you start," Ms. Lang said.

"Okay," Lily said. "I'm Lily, and, um, I can help you

with your class schedule. It can look kind of confusing at first because every day is different."

"Thanks, Lily," Ms. Lang said. "Great idea. Olivia?"

"I'm Olivia, and I can help you with your locker," Olivia said. "In case you can't open it or something. And if you want, I can help you decorate the inside. Most kids put some stuff up inside to sort of personalize it. Like, everything in mine is purple."

Now it was Lissa's turn. "I'm Lissa, and I can help you find the right bus to go home on today," she said.

"Oh, thanks, but that's easy," Bethany said. "My bus is bus number two. It goes right by the graveyard. My new house is right next to the graveyard."

"I know!" Lissa said enthusiastically. "I live on the other side of the graveyard. My brother told me about you. You're my new neighbor!"

Ms. Lang smiled. "You two should finish this conversation after we've gone all the way around the circle. But it's great that you're neighbors. Kier?"

"I'm Kier, and I can help you with the lunch line," Kier said. "The food is pretty gross, and I can help you choose the good stuff." Everyone laughed, and Lissa and Bethany smiled at each other.

After everyone finished going around the circle, homeroom was soon over, and everyone went their own ways to class. Lissa had math with Olivia, Lily went off to English, and Bethany had history. Lissa and Olivia pointed her in the right direction.

The history teacher, Mr. Parmalee, was one of the seventh graders' favorite teachers. He was young and cool, and made the subject interesting even to kids who claimed to hate it. They did projects like researching their own family trees, exploring the history of their own house and neighborhood, and interviewing senior citizens about historical events like the Great Depression and World War II. Like Lissa and Nate's parents, he was extremely interested in local history.

Mr. Parmalee saw Bethany and gave her a friendly hello and showed her where to sit. It happened to be right next to Nate, who was also in this class. Bethany gave Nate a sidelong glance. He was shaking his hair out of his eyes in a really cool way.

"Hey," Bethany said to him. She got a better look at him and noticed his dimples. *He's just as cute as he was on my porch!* she thought. But what she said instead was, "I just met your sister. Let me guess, you're twins?"

"Ding, ding, ding!" Nate said, as if Bethany had just gotten an answer correct on a game show, and they both laughed.

"We're the two and only," he added. Nate was pleased he'd said something sort of clever, to make up for his awkwardness yesterday. *She's even prettier than I realized,* he thought, trying hard not to stare.

"Okay, everyone, the unit of study you've all been waiting for," Mr. Parmalee said. "The history of your own hometown, Old Warwick."

Everyone was ready for this. Mr. Parmalee was famous for this unit, which explored the history of their town from its very beginning to the present. It included a field trip to the Old Warwick Historical Society and the graveyard next to Nate and Lissa's. The kids always made rubbings of the gravestones, which was more fun than it sounded.

"I could teach this unit for you if you like," Nate joked. Everyone, especially Mr. Parmalee, knew where Nate lived and what his parents did.

"Well, your parents certainly could," Mr. Parmalee

said. "Perhaps we should have them in as guest speakers." Nate looked like a deer in headlights.

"Kidding! I'm kidding," Mr. Parmalee reassured him. "But if it wasn't such a horrifying idea for you, I'd be tempted to include your home in the field trip. I hear your parents have done an amazing job with the historical restoration."

"Stop! Just stop!" Nate had his head down on his desk. Everyone laughed.

Mr. Parmalee passed out reading and activity packets to begin the unit. "Now, what do you already know about Old Warwick?"

"It's named for Lord and Lady Warwick, the original founders," someone said.

"Righto," Mr. Parmalee said. "And where did they come here from?"

"England," someone else said.

"Right again," said Mr. Parmalee. "Who remembers when?"

"The 1600s," someone else said.

"And why did they leave and come here?" Mr. Parmalee probed.

"The Puritans were fleeing religious persecution in

England," Bethany said. She already knew this from history class at her old school.

"Good," Mr. Parmalee said. "You guys already know the basics. What else do you know?"

"Nate's house is right next to a graveyard haunted by Lady Warwick," someone else said, and everyone laughed again.

"Um, well, the same could be said for me, if that were true," Bethany said. "What's up with that?"

"Ah, the legend of Lady Warwick." Mr. Parmalee sighed. "You guys know that's just a ghost story, right? But I'm sure you want to have a quick recap for fun. Who wants to share it with our newcomer?" A few kids raised their hands.

"We might as well hear it from the expert," Mr. Parmalee said, gesturing to Nate. A few kids laughed, and Nate grinned.

"Okay, here's how it goes," Nate began. "Lady and Lord Warwick moved here, and soon after, Lady Warwick died after some mysterious illness. Lord Warwick buried her in their yard. But when he moved, he wanted her grave moved too, so they dug her up. When they opened the coffin, the inside was full of scratch marks. Because she had been accidentally buried alive. And there was no skeleton there." He paused for effect. He had heard this story many times before, of course.

"And now, they say when you hear the windows rattling or branches scratching at your window, it's Lady Warwick trying to get back in, trying to reunite with her beloved Lord Warwick. And also, she's crazy and heartbroken. She's been roaming the woods all this time."

"I know it's just a story, but the end always gives me shivers," one girl said.

"A ghost story can be fun," Mr. Parmalee said. "But everyone remember it's just a local legend, told and retold over the years to scare people."

"Especially the guests at my parents' B and B," Nate said sarcastically. "That story is framed above our staircase."

Bethany flashed a smile. "Maybe I should get a copy for our house too. No wonder that graveyard is so quiet and overgrown. Everyone's scared to go in." She couldn't help but notice Nate was staring at her.

Next up was math, which Bethany and Nate also had together. It was easy for Bethany; she'd already covered the material in her previous school in New York City. When it was time to work on problems with partners, she even helped Nate. Again, she felt his eyes on her the whole time. He struggled to pay attention to what she was saying, so he could finish the problems himself, but it was difficult. She was so pretty and easy to talk to. Nate had never met a girl like her before.

On the bus on the way home, Lissa found a seat next to Bethany. Nate had soccer practice, so he wasn't on the bus. Lissa and Bethany got off the bus together and looked at each other.

"There's my house, of course," Bethany said, and pointed.

Lissa laughed. "There's my house, of course," she said. "I'm so glad a kid moved in there. Mr. Reiney was nice, but there was never any fun in the neighborhood."

"Ta-da!" Bethany said, and threw her arms up in the air. They both cracked up.

"Hey, the Warwick Inn," Bethany said, seeing the sign. "Cool."

"Kind of," Lissa said. "But not really, you know?"

"Really? I think it would be so fun to live in a B and B. My parents like to stay in them sometimes. I like the breakfasts," Bethany said. "They're always really big."

"Well, you'll love our place, then," Lissa said. "Hey, Olivia and Lily are coming for a sleepover on Friday. Why don't you come too?"

"I'd love to," Bethany said without hesitating. Lissa was impressed by her confidence. She wasn't sure that she'd have been able to make new friends so quickly at a new school. But Bethany just seemed so at ease.

CHAPTER 4

Spring had finally sprung in Old Warwick. The magnolia tree in front of Lissa and Nate's house was in full bloom as Olivia marched happily down the path leading to the front door. She was carrying her purple backpack and her pillow in its purple pillowcase.

Lissa has adored Olivia ever since first grade, when their class went on a field trip to the American Museum of Natural History and Lissa had gotten scared of the big dinosaur. Other kids were giggling because Lissa was afraid, but Olivia quietly took her hand as they all walked by the giant creature. Olivia also never made fun of Lissa for sleeping with a teddy bear or being afraid of birds that swooped too close to her head.

Olivia was the most rational and logical of the three

of them, and the least likely to get spooked by ghost stories, which made her the perfect person to sleep next to at sleepovers. No matter what Lissa told her mom, the truth was, they *did* tell ghost stories sometimes.

Moments later Lily arrived, her mom dropping her off in the driveway with a wave good-bye. Lily was the most naive of the three, the most likely to get spooked by ghost stories, and also the only one of the three who didn't roll her eyes at the Lady Warwick ghost story. She seemed to believe it wholeheartedly and took it very seriously. Lily even avoided the framed story about Lady Warwick hanging in the entranceway, claiming, "I think it's probably bad luck to even *read* about her!"

Lily had made friends with Olivia right away when she arrived in town in fourth grade, but Lissa didn't really get to know her until fifth grade. It was later that summer that they had begun their tradition of burying each other in sand after the school year ended. This year would be the third annual "Sandy Lady" ritual at the beach. Nate laughed at the Sandy Lady ritual, but the girls thought his hobby of fishing off the pier was equally lame. Lame *and* gross, according to Lissa.

It was seven p.m., the sun hadn't set, and the girls hadn't eaten dinner. Neither had Nate, so the Carlsons ordered pizza: one pepperoni and one plain, since Olivia had recently become a vegetarian. As they waited for the pizza to arrive, they used their phones to take pictures of one another climbing the big tree in the front yard.

It was an excellent tree, and while Lissa had loved climbing it and playing in it when she was little, these days it was more of a photo op tree. The pictures were artsy and cool, and the girls took turns looking at one another's photos and laughing. The best was one of Lissa and Lily hanging upside down off a low branch, their hair hanging down strangely.

"So Bethany will be here soon," Lissa told Olivia and Lily. "You're sure that's okay? I didn't really ask you guys about it before I invited her. It just seemed like the right thing to do at the time."

"Totally," Olivia said. "I really like her. And she's your next-door neighbor, after all."

"And Nate's in love with her," Lily added immediately. Olivia and Lissa stared at her in disbelief.

"No, really," Lily said. "It was ridiculously obvious

all week in school. He can't stop staring at her. I can't believe you guys didn't notice."

Lissa frowned. "First of all, *ew*," she said. "My brother is gross. Second of all, I don't keep tabs on him all day."

"Whatever," Lily said. "I can see why Nate would like her. She's really pretty, and she's smart and funny. What's the big deal?"

"It's not a big deal," Lissa and Olivia said at the same time, and then both laughed. A moment later they saw Bethany and her parents approaching from the sidewalk.

"Hey!" they called. Bethany gave a little wave and smiled. Her long, curly hair bounced around her shoulders, and she wore pink lip gloss that made her look very glamorous. Her parents went to knock on the door to meet Lissa's parents, who opened their door with a smile and let their new neighbors in. They already had lemonade and cookies set out for them.

"Welcome to the neighborhood!" Mr. Carlson said. "I'm Ed Carlson, and this is my wife, Linda. We're so happy to meet you, and glad the girls made friends so quickly."

"Richard Warren. Pleasure to meet you," Bethany's dad said. "And this is Sally," he added, indicating

Bethany's mom. The four stood in the kitchen smiling at one another.

"So where are you from, and what brings you to our fair port?" Mr. Carlson asked the Warrens.

"We're from Manhattan," Mr. Warren said. "My marketing firm is opening a new office in New Haven. They sent me here to get it going. And Sally here writes for an advertising firm, and she's going to commute to the city three days a week, and write at home the other two days."

The Carlsons nodded attentively.

Mr. Warren continued, "We're both going to be out of the house a lot for the next few months while we settle things with our jobs. My aunt is living with us. She's helping to look after Bethany on the days when Sally and I have to stay over in the city. We're trying to keep those days few and far between, but we probably won't be around as much as we'd like for a while. We're really hoping things settle down this summer!"

Mrs. Warren added, "Luckily, Bethany is very resilient and has been a really good sport about all this."

"She seems like a lovely girl," Mrs. Carlson agreed. "And she's always welcome here! Would you like a tour of the B and B?"

"Absolutely," Mrs. Warren said. They started by the staircase, where Mrs. Carlson pointed out the framed ghost story. Mr. and Mrs. Warren leaned in to read it.

"Spooky!" Mrs. Warren said with a little shiver. "Was there really a Lady Warwick?"

"Oh, absolutely," said Mr. Carlson. "And if you listen closely at night, you might hear her tapping at *your* windows too, since you're just on the other side of the cemetery!"

The adults laughed in appreciation of Mr. Carlson's joke and then headed upstairs for the rest of the tour.

While their parents talked inside, Lissa got to the important matter at hand. "We ordered pizza," she told Bethany.

"Excellent," Bethany said. "I *love* pizza!"

Just then the pizza arrived. Nate loped down to the kitchen to join them and grabbed a piece of pepperoni, stuffing it into his mouth without even taking a plate. "Where are you rushing off to?" Lissa asked. But Nate didn't answer.

The night wore on, and Nate continued to avoid the girls. He didn't even join them when they made their cookie dough like he usually did. He did, however, come out to eat some of it after Lissa made a point of inviting him to join them.

Maybe Lily's right and he does have a crush on Bethany, Lissa thought. It would certainly explain her brother's strange behavior.

"You have a little flour on your face," was the first thing he said to Bethany. Lissa brushed it off for her, and they all laughed.

When everyone came off their sugar high, the girls settled into Lissa's room for the night. Nate had wandered off without saying good night. Lissa quickly spread out her sleeping bag and sat cross-legged on the floor as Olivia, Lily, and Bethany unrolled their sleeping bags.

"Ouch!" Bethany cried suddenly, her hands on her foot. "What was that?"

Everyone laughed. "Sorry, that's Howard," Lissa said.

"What? Who?" Bethany seemed panicked, and the girls laughed even harder.

"Howard the cat," Lissa explained quickly. "He ambushes people's feet."

She reached under the bed and pulled out a long, sleek black cat with pretty yellow eyes. She held him in her arms, her face close to his as she cooed lovingly, "You're an ambusher, aren't you, Howard? Can you please not ambush the newcomer? Thanks, I'd appreciate it." She let him down, and he scurried right back under the bed, ready to ambush again.

They all got into their sleeping bags and turned out the light. But no one was ready for sleep.

"Let's interview Bethany," Olivia suggested. "Like the interviews we did in history class. Everyone gets to ask her a question."

Bethany giggled. "Sure, as long as I can reserve the right not to answer," she said.

"We'll go easy on you," Lissa assured her. "Okay, I'll start. Do you like Old Warwick so far?"

Bethany answered right away. "Sure. It's really different from New York City, though. It's much quieter. But I like living at the beach, and school's okay so far."

Now it was Olivia's turn. "Who's in your family?" she asked.

"Well, I'm an only child," Bethany said. "My parents are working a lot, and my aunt Mimi lives with us. She's supposed to keep an eye on me when they're not around, but she's getting a little forgetful. She's, like, not even that old yet, but she's starting to have problems with her memory."

"My grandmother had that," Lissa said, nodding sympathetically.

Now it was Lily's turn. "Do you think Nate is cute?" she asked boldly.

In the dark, no one could see Bethany's shy smile. "I reserve the right not to answer," she said slyly.

"That means you think he is!" Lily crowed.

"Well, I sort of had a boyfriend in New York, and *he* was really cute," Bethany said, trying to change the subject.

"Really?" Lily asked. "Were you devastated to leave him?"

"Whatever . . . we just went to the movies a few times. It's not like I was going to marry him. I spent most of my free time with my friends. I had three best friends, and we've been friends since preschool," Bethany said. "I miss *them* more than him," she added, a note of sadness in her voice.

"I bet," Lily said. "I can't imagine having to move away from Olivia and Lissa. Okay, well, here's another question. It's different from the last one. Do you think Nate is *hot*?"

"You're unbelievable!" Bethany laughed. "Okay, fine.

He's really cute. But this is a girls' night, right? We don't need to talk about boys. Hey, how about *I* interview *you* guys?"

But suddenly they were all startled by a loud scratching at the window. It sounded like branches tapping and rubbing against the window—but there were no trees outside Lissa's room.

"Lady Warwick!" Lily screamed, and the three other girls immediately started shrieking along with her.

CHAPTER 5

The next morning Lissa, Olivia, and Bethany were embarrassed over their outburst. But Lily remained spooked. "It was Lady Warwick!" she insisted. But after saying it a few times in the bright daylight of the kitchen as they munched on waffles, even Lily had to admit that *maybe* they had overreacted.

Then Nate wandered in and asked them what all the screaming the night before was about.

"We heard scratching at the windows!" Lissa and Olivia said at the same time, and then they all cracked up.

"Maybe it was Lady You-Know-Who trying to get in," Nate said, casually drizzling honey on his waffle. Lissa noticed he seemed to keep one eye on Bethany to see if she was frightened or not.

Bethany saw him looking at her and smiled shyly.

"I'm off to the beach. Bye, screamers," Nate said to the girls. He proudly held up his metal detector and waved it like a sword.

"Off to hunt for buried treasure?" Lissa asked sarcastically.

Nate was cute and popular, but Lissa felt he definitely had a weird side. He loved to go to tag sales with their mother, which Lissa thought was about the lamest thing imaginable. But Nate secretly felt that going tagging was the most fun you could have. Each tag sale was like its own little treasure hunt, and everything was so inexpensive. Sure, there was a lot of junk, too, but as his grandmother used to say, "One man's junk is another man's treasure."

Like, for instance, the metal detector that he had bought at a tag sale last summer. It was quite old, probably from the 1980s, and his mother had explained that you used it to hunt for buried treasure on the beach. It looked like a cane with sort of a Frisbee at the end of it. You held the Frisbee part to the ground, and the machine beeped when it detected metal. The metal could be a piece of foil, a coin, or a piece of jewelry.

Who knew when you'd come upon a real find?

Nate had been taking his metal detector to the beach regularly, stopping only in the dead of winter when there was too much snow on the ground. So far he had found a bunch of coins, an earring, and a watch. And lots of bottle caps and tin cans. And, of course, that one piece of buried treasure, the ruby ring.

That night Bethany wrote in her journal.

It was a fun sleepover at Lissa's. I'm lucky to have made friends so fast. I make friends pretty easily, but still. The setup is good, with my place and Lissa's being practically next door to each other. Except that old town graveyard in between, of course! It doesn't spook me like people might think. I'm just not that easy to spook. Anyway . . . we had pizza, and Nate didn't talk to me that much, but I think he likes me. Lily thinks so too. She asked me if I thought he was cute.

Then there was this crazy tapping at the window that scared everyone. Lily was the most scared. Some town ghost story or something that everyone's obsessed with, though they claim not to be! We're even studying it in history class.

Well, I do think he is cute. That's my answer. I kind of hope he does like me.

Anyway, we made cookie dough, which I had never eaten raw before, but it was totally delicious, and they interviewed me, which was kind of fun, and I got ambushed by Howard the cat. All in all, an excellent sleepover.

Oh. I forgot to write anything about school, ha-ha! It's fine. Nate and I are in history and math together. In history I heard that the graveyard between my place and the Carlsons' place is haunted. But I don't believe it!

CHAPTER 6

The week in school went quickly. Bethany seemed to sail through her classes. When the girls asked her about it, she modestly explained that she had covered a lot of the material already at her old school.

Though Lissa didn't have history class with Nate and Bethany, they had the same unit in local history and the same homework. They were each supposed to choose an aspect of colonial life in Old Warwick that they wanted to explore for the rest of the semester. Lissa chose food, her favorite topic. Nate chose town government, Bethany chose the role of women in colonial life, Olivia chose religion, and Lily chose professions. When they were finished with their research, they would each give a presentation to the class.

All week, Lissa researched colonial food. She had to admit a lot of it didn't seem too appetizing. Salt pork! She was glad she'd been born when she was. The major similarity she found between now and then was that people would fish for food. *Nate would have been right at home back then,* Lissa thought. *He totally thinks he's a real fisherman when he's on the pier, even though he never catches anything!*

Another Friday night, another sleepover, Lissa thought happily as she helped her mom make spaghetti sauce. The two chopped onions and talked.

"You'll love this, Mom," Lissa said, wiping the tears from her eyes. The onions were making them water like crazy. "We started the unit on local history in class."

"Finally!" said her mom, smiling widely. "I bet you'll love it too. It includes a field trip to the graveyard at the end of the year, right?"

"Yup," Lissa said. "And the historical society museum."

Her mom could barely contain her pleasure. "Do they need chaperones?"

"You wish." Lissa grinned. "Bethany's researching the role of women in colonial Old Warwick," she went on as she finished the onions and moved on to the zucchini.

"Oh, that sounds so interesting," her mom said as she sautéed the onions. "I'll have to ask her about that. And how about you, miss?"

"Food, of course!" Lissa said.

"Really?" her mom asked. "That's neat. What about your brother?"

"Government, of course!"

"Of course." Mrs. Carlson smiled. "Nate's getting more and more interested in politics, isn't he? You know, we have some old Yankee cookbooks in the B and B library if you'd like to use them in your research. Hey, I have a great idea. If you give me a list of things that the early settlers made, based on your finished research, we'll make a special menu of them for the guests."

Lissa rolled her eyes. "I'm doing research online. Anyway, I don't think many of the guests would like salt pork!" She laughed. "But maybe a fish dinner would work. Speaking of dinner, Bethany, Lily, and Olivia are coming at seven, so they'll be eating with us, okay?"

"Sure," her mom said. "So what's Bethany like?"

"She's great," Lissa said. "She's kind of a city kid, but she's not snobby about it. She has cool clothes and seems to know everything we're learning in school because she already learned most of it at her old school. But she's really nice. Lily and Olivia think so too. Oh, and it's her birthday on Sunday."

"Are you going to make her a cookie dough cake?" her mom joked.

"Actually, yes," Lissa said. "And we got her red lip gloss because she likes to wear lip gloss. She usually wears pink, but we found this cool red color that's supposed to taste like strawberries, and I happen to know she loves strawberries."

"That's sweet," her mom said, adding a large can of chopped tomatoes and some big pinches of Italian seasoning to the sauce. "I'm sure she'll like that."

Everyone lined up in the kitchen to help themselves to the big bowl of pasta and the giant steaming pot of sauce on the stove.

"Everyone *must* love this sauce," announced Lissa. "Because I made it."

"You and *Mom* made it," Nate corrected her.

"True," Lissa said. "But notice how beautifully the vegetables are chopped. That's my handiwork right there."

"They *are* quite beautiful," said Bethany.

They took their plates to the table. Once everyone had their big piles of spaghetti in front of them, they all dug in.

"Olivia and Lily, you know about our Friday night tradition whenever we sit down together, right?" Mr. Carlson asked.

"Where everyone says a good thing about this past week?" Olivia asked, impaling a large chunk of zucchini on her fork.

"Right. We go around the table," Mr. Carlson said. "I'll start. The highlight of my week was driving up to Hartford for an antique show and finding the perfect small table for one of the guest rooms."

Mrs. Carlson smiled. "You really love those antique shows, don't you, Ed? Okay, mine was picking all the basil I've been growing in the garden and using it in this sauce, which I must admit came out really well." Everyone nodded in agreement.

"It's really good, Mrs. Carlson," Bethany said with a smile.

It was Nate's turn. He and Lissa both thought the go-around-the-table thing was kind of corny, but they'd been doing it since they were little, and they secretly kind of liked it. "Mine was deciding I'm going to run for class president," he said casually.

His parents put their forks down. "Wow!" they said in unison. "That's wonderful, Nate!"

This was news to Lissa and her friends, but it made sense. Nate was a natural leader, and all different groups of kids in school liked him. He also said he wanted to major in political science when he went to college. His parents always reminded him he didn't have to choose so soon, but he'd been insisting for a few years now.

"We can help you make signs," Bethany said.

"Really? Thanks," Nate said, smiling and suddenly looking very closely at his spaghetti.

"Okay, me!" Lissa said. "The spring dance was announced this week." She added to the girls, "I can't wait till we all get our dresses together."

"That was my favorite thing this week too," Olivia said.

"Me too," added Lily. "What about you, Bethany?"

"Um, that too, but also, it's my birthday week, so my parents give me one little present every day leading up to Sunday, and I got some cool stuff," she said. "Also, well, I was really happy to be invited for another sleepover." Her smile was, uncharacteristically, slightly shy.

After dinner, it was time for making cookie dough. On tonight's menu was peanut butter cookie dough. When they'd finished mixing it up, Lissa, Olivia, and Lily rolled a big gob of it into a perfect ball, put it on a plate, pressed a fork into it twice to make a crisscross pattern in the center, and presented it to Bethany with one lit candle stuck in. As they sang "Happy Birthday," Bethany sang along happily, substituting "Happy birthday, dear me" for "Happy birthday, dear Bethany."

"And that's not all," Lissa told her. "Here. From the three of us." She handed Bethany a little gift bag.

"Oh, you didn't have to get me a present!" Bethany cried. But they could all tell how happy she was about it.

"Oh, I love this color!" she said as she examined the tube of red lip gloss. She put some on right away and smiled widely, then blew each of her new friends a kiss. It made her lips bright, shiny red.

"I think I've found my new signature color!" she said,

looking in the mirror. "I actually love this red so much more than pink. Thanks, you guys!"

In Lissa's room, as the girls were getting ready for bed, Bethany pulled her pajamas out of her backpack and saw something shiny come flying out. "Wait, what was that?" she said. She felt around on the rug.

"It's a ring!" she exclaimed, pulling it out from where it had landed under the bed. "But it's not mine." She sounded puzzled.

"It was definitely in your bag," Lily said.

"I know, but it's not mine," Bethany repeated.

Lily was grinning. "I bet Nate hid it in your bag."

Olivia, Lily, and Lissa all exchanged looks.

"Oh yeah," Lissa said, nodding. "It was definitely Nate. He loves hiding presents. He does it all the time for our birthdays!"

"Did you see him put it there?" Bethany asked her. She put the ring on her finger and stared at it, moving her hand very close to her eyes, then farther away.

"No, but trust me," Lissa said, laughing. "It's totally from him. He knew it was your birthday!"

"You really think it came from him?" Bethany asked the girls, who were all giggling. Bethany really wanted the ring to be from Nate, but she needed to be sure.

"Duh, we thought you were pretty smart," Olivia said. "Don't tell me you haven't noticed the way he stares at you. Or tries not to stare at you, to be more precise."

Bethany couldn't help but blush. "I guess I have," she admitted. "But where did he get it? It looks expensive and old."

"Probably at one of his tag sales," Lissa said. "He loves going to those with my mom."

Bethany wiggled her finger and continued to admire the ring. She thought it looked perfect on her hand, like it belonged there. *I've never even owned a ring before,* she thought happily, almost transfixed by how pretty and sparkly the little ruby was.

It was, by far, the best present she'd ever been given.

CHAPTER 7

The next morning at breakfast, Bethany was wearing both of her presents: her red lip gloss and her ruby ring. She explained to Mr. and Mrs. Carlson how she had mysteriously found the ring in her bag.

"It's beautiful!" Mrs. Carlson exclaimed, admiring it between sips of coffee. "It looks very old."

Nate looked casually at the ring, as if he had never seen it before.

"You know," he said thoughtfully, "Lady Warwick herself wore a ruby ring." Everyone laughed, and Bethany laughed along.

"You know what else?" Nate said. "She had ruby-red lips, too." Bethany stared at him as the other three girls exchanged knowing looks. Nate was definitely flirting.

"Another scone, milady?" he asked her, passing the scone basket to her. *My lady.* Bethany was still staring at him.

Lissa and Lily giggled, and Olivia rolled her eyes, as if this romantic, old-fashioned exchange was kind of grossing her out.

And Nate was nowhere near finished with this routine. "Now that you're Lady Warwick, I shall be Lord Warwick!" he proclaimed, holding his spoon straight up in the air as if in official announcement mode.

"This scone is delicious, milord." Bethany smiled and made a gesture that looked like a curtsy, even though she was sitting down. She took a big bite of scone and laughed daintily.

"Okay, Lord Warwick," Mrs. Carlson said to Nate. "Grab your things. We've got to get you to Your Lordship's soccer game."

And then Nate did the most astonishing thing. He stood with a flourish, walked over to where Bethany sat, took her hand, and kissed the ring in a grand, fancy gesture, which made all four girls go completely silent. But then, moments later, they dissolved into giggles.

Bethany really liked history class. It was great timing that had her studying the history of the town as soon as she'd moved there, and she liked the research topic she had chosen, the role of women in colonial life.

Today was her turn to share her "top five" points about her research topic. She stood in front of the group and tried not to read directly from her paper. As she spoke, Nate noticed she was twirling the ring around her finger. She had it on her left ring finger, the finger a wedding ring is supposed to go on. Bethany was actually a little glad her parents were spending the whole week in Manhattan. She purposely hadn't worn the ring when they took her out to dinner for her birthday on Sunday night. It made her sad to take it off, but she didn't want to explain to her parents where it had come from. At least, not yet. She was pretty sure she'd be able to hide it from them until they got used to her having a boyfriend. In the meantime, she was sure Aunt Mimi wouldn't notice her wearing it.

But now she was happy to have it on her finger again, for all to see.

"My topic is the role of women in colonial life. Let me first say that women have it much better in today's society. Early colonial life was hard for women. There were more men than women in the settlement of Old Warwick, so the women who were there had an extra burden to carry." The rest of the class took notes.

"Second, here is what women did in Old Warwick: They raised children, sewed, cooked, took care of animals, made soap, made candles, made clothes, and did all the other housework while men fished, built, plowed, harvested, hunted, and protected the family from wild animals and Indians."

"That's the way it should be!" one boy said, and a few kids laughed.

Mr. Parmalee stopped the joking before it got out of hand. "And I'm not sure any of you boys would be too keen on protecting your homes from wild animals, either. I apologize for the boorish behavior of these boys, Bethany. Please continue."

Bethany smiled. "Third, the colonists brought with them very traditional attitudes about the status and roles of women. Women were considered to be 'weaker vessels,' not as strong physically or mentally as men, and less emotionally stable," she continued. After Mr. Parmalee's last warning, nobody was going to touch that one.

"Fourth, women could not vote or hold public office. And fifth, women were expected to be obedient to their husbands without question."

She was done. She smiled and gave her ring another twist as she sat down.

"Thank you, Bethany. That was very illuminating," Mr. Parmalee said.

After class, Nate approached Bethany on their way to lunch. "Nice job," he said.

"Thanks," she said. She got butterflies in her stomach when he talked to her now. She used to feel normal around him, but after Saturday's scone incident, she felt all tingly inside. She also couldn't stop staring at his dimples.

"So how do you like your ruby ring, milady?" he asked shyly.

"I love it, milord," she responded just as shyly. She held her head low and looked up at him. Then she got brave.

"Thank you for giving it to me," she said, looking right into his eyes.

"You're welcome," he said. And there it was. She promised herself she would never take the ring off.

That night, in bed in her pajamas, Bethany wrote in her journal:

Well, the ring is definitely from none other than Nate, who shall from now on be referred to here as milord. Get it, my lord? Because I am his lady. (He calls me milady, how cute is that?) I can't believe this is happening.

I did my report on the role of women in Old Warwick yesterday. It went pretty well. It's funny, when I first started my research, I thought it sounded like the women of Old Warwick had it SO bad. But I've changed my mind. The idea of cooking and quilting all day actually seems kind of nice. I imagine me as Lady Warwick and Nate as Lord Warwick, and our little colonial house, with smoke coming from the chimney. I'd bake some corn bread for him to enjoy when he got home from fishing. And I'd fry up the fish he caught. Yum!

This has been such a weird day. I was so happy in school when Nate and I talked and I thanked him for the ring. I know he really likes me, but tonight I keep thinking he's going to change his mind about me and start liking someone else. I don't know what I would do if that happened. I would just be heartbroken.

But that is totally ridiculous. Why am I worrying so much? And this insecure feeling is so not me. I just need to keep looking at my beautiful ring and remind myself of that.

Then Bethany fell asleep. And a few hours later, she woke up suddenly to a loud *yowl*. And something scratching at her feet.

She opened her eyes and couldn't believe it. She was standing up, first of all.

Second of all, she was standing in front of Nate and Lissa's house. In her pajamas.

Third of all, Howard had ambushed her feet again and was running away to hide in the bushes.

She had been sleepwalking . . . which had never happened to her before.

The Carlsons' house was completely dark. As was the whole sky. Bethany could barely see a thing.

Once she caught her breath and realized what had happened, her first thought was, *Oh my God. I'm so glad no one saw me! They would think I was some kind of stalker.*

She began to walk home.

I hope this doesn't happen again, she said to herself over and over, a horrible feeling in the pit of her stomach.

This is crazy. I am so glad Mom and Dad aren't home and that Aunt Mimi is such a deep sleeper. With that, Bethany hurried back to her home and tried to fall back asleep. But she barely slept a wink for the rest of the night.

CHAPTER 8

A few weeks later, it was finally time for end-of-school-year elections. Bethany's parents had returned home, and Bethany had not had any more sleepwalking incidents. She'd kept the whole thing a secret. Now her parents were out of town again, but they had promised this would probably be the last time. Bethany didn't mind too much. When the Carlsons heard that her parents were away, they practically insisted she spend as much time as possible at their house. And Bethany definitely didn't mind that!

She was there now, as were Lily and Olivia. The girls helped Nate make a ton of "Vote for Nate" posters. Their slogans were "Nate the Great," "Turn Over a New Leaf with Nate" (decorated with fall leaves), and "Nate Carlson, the People's President" (decorated with color copies of yearbook photos of every student in their class). The "People's President" one had been Bethany's idea.

"It's important that every kid feel like he or she is part of Nate's presidency, like they each have a voice," she pointed out. It seemed like a great idea, and she happily glued the individual photos, collage-style, onto those posters.

"I can't believe how much work you guys are doing on these," Nate said, wandering into the kitchen, where the girls had set up a whole poster-making workshop. He was talking to all four girls, but his eyes were on Bethany. He picked up a marker and began coloring in the bubble letters on one of the posters.

Bethany held up her glitter pen and reached over and touched his nose with it so he had a sparkly nose. "Of course we are, milord." The others rolled their eyes.

"You know, Lord Warwick became the first governor of Old Warwick," he said. "That's a sneak preview of my report in history. And history repeats itself, doesn't it?"

"It does, milord," Bethany said, sounding awfully old-fashioned, and Nate blushed.

Lissa exchanged a look with Olivia and Lily. *This is*

really annoying, the look said. The three girls had secretly discussed that they thought Bethany and Nate were taking this "milord, milady" thing a bit too far. "She was talking about learning to cook fish in case he ever catches any!" Lissa had said to Olivia and Lily in exasperation. "I mean, seriously? Is she for real?"

As if she somehow knew what her friends were thinking, Bethany excused herself and went into the bathroom. Lissa immediately felt guilty for thinking disloyal thoughts about her friend and shared a tense, nervous look with the other girls.

But then Bethany called to her friends from the bathroom. "Hey, you guys! Come here!"

"Lookit," she said, indicating her hair, which was parted straight down the middle. "Why didn't you tell me my hair looked like this?"

"I thought maybe you were going for a seventies look," Lissa said, and they all laughed.

"Oh yuck," Bethany said, and made a face in the mirror as she fixed her hair. "My hair has been acting totally bizarro lately! You have to tell me if it does that again!"

"Why, are you worried Nate won't like it?" Lily teased. Olivia and Lissa paused, unsure of how Bethany would react. But she just made a funny face in the mirror, and all four girls cracked up laughing together.

The tension, it seemed, had passed.

There was a week of campaigning before the elections, and Nate's posters looked better than any other candidate's. His speech at the class assembly went perfectly. It was all about how he cared about the concerns of each and every student in the class, and how anyone could come talk to him anytime about any question or problem. He said that even if he didn't win the election, he felt proud to be a member of the class and valued his relationship with every single one of his classmates.

After the assembly with the speeches, Bethany and Lissa walked to lunch to meet Olivia and Lily at their usual table.

"Nate did great, right?" Lily said right away.

"Totally," Olivia and Lissa said at the same time.

"Whatever," Bethany said quickly. "Next topic." They all looked shocked by her comment.

"Where did that come from?" Lissa said, opening her bag of baby carrots.

"Sorry," Bethany said. "I didn't mean to sound harsh. It's just that, well, I didn't really like what he said about *each and every* kid being able to talk to him *anytime* about *anything*."

"Why not?" asked Lily. "It seems like a good thing to say in a speech like that."

"Yeah, but that means other girls can call him any-time," Bethany said, as if that should have been obvious to the others.

Lissa, Olivia, and Lily couldn't help but laugh. "You're a jealous girlfriend!" Lily cried.

Bethany sighed. "I know. And I don't know what's the matter with me."

CHAPTER 9

Nate won the election. He was going to be class president.

Their school always had the spring dance right after elections, and the new class officers—president, vice president, secretary, treasurer—all appeared at a sort of "welcoming" line as kids entered. It was the beginning of their formal duties as class officers. Nate had his tuxedo ready (the officers got more dressed up than the other kids), and the girls had done their dress shopping at the mall. They were each pleased with their decisions, except Bethany, who had seemed sullen and withdrawn and hated everything she tried on. She left the mall without buying anything.

"What's the matter, Bethany?" Olivia had asked when they were all in the dressing room.

"Nate hasn't asked me yet," Bethany replied, her eyes filling with tears. "And the dance is *next weekend*!" The others were shocked to see her so upset.

"Maybe because he's president, he feels like the dance isn't really for having fun at," Lissa offered gently, touching Bethany's arm. "Maybe he feels like it's part of his presidential duties and he has a responsibility to the whole class or something." Lissa hadn't really thought of this before, but it sort of made sense, and she was trying to help Bethany feel better.

"Yeah, maybe," Bethany said, but she didn't sound too convinced.

Mrs. Carlson picked them up soon after, and the four girls left the mall with three dresses. They went back to Lissa's, where Mr. Carlson and Nate were sitting on the front porch drinking iced tea.

"Well, let's see those dresses," Mrs. Carlson said. Lissa, Olivia, and Lily all pulled their dresses out of their bags and held them up. As the Carlsons admired them, Bethany suddenly bolted from the porch, ran home, and went straight into her bedroom.

She threw herself onto her bed, where she cried and cried. *Maybe he's taking someone else to the dance,* she thought over and over again. She couldn't stop thinking it. Until she heard the doorbell ring and her aunt Mimi answer it.

Aunt Mimi appeared at her door moments later. "Bethany, there's a young man here to see you. His name is Nate."

"Okay," Bethany said, smiling through her tears. She stopped crying and went to the bathroom to splash her face. After doing so, she looked in the mirror and realized he'd be able to tell right away that she'd been crying. *That's okay, maybe women really are weaker vessels, not as strong psychologically as men,* she thought, remembering her history report. She applied her red lip gloss and fixed her hair (which had parted itself in the middle AGAIN!) and headed downstairs.

When she got downstairs, Nate was standing in the doorway.

"Why did you run off?" he asked kindly. "Why didn't you get a dress like the others did?"

"I guess I wasn't sure I was going," she said neutrally.

"Aren't you going to go with me, milady?" Nate asked, incredulous.

"Well, you haven't exactly *asked* me," Bethany pointed

out, trying to keep the relieved smile off her face.

Nate's face fell. "I'm really sorry, milady. I just assumed!" he exclaimed. "You need a formal invitation, do you, milady?"

"I suppose I do, milord," Bethany said demurely.

Nate ducked his head. He seemed suddenly shy. "Will you go to the dance with me, milady?"

"Yes, milord," Bethany said, and smiled so hard she thought her face would break.

CHAPTER 10

A few days later, the night of the big dance arrived. The girls got ready together in Lissa's room, Bethany borrowing a red dress of Lissa's that perfectly matched her ruby ring. They did one another's hair. Olivia, who was a whiz with hairdos, came up with a pretty updo that actually worked well with the middle part that Bethany's hair seemed to be stubbornly falling into.

"That dress really makes your ring stand out," Lissa told Bethany, and Bethany's face lit up.

Once they emerged from Lissa's room, Mr. and Mrs. Carlson were eagerly awaiting them with cameras. Nate still hadn't come downstairs, but that didn't stop them from snapping away.

"You're like the paparazzi!" Lissa complained, but she

didn't really mind. Then Nate appeared in his tuxedo.

"Spiffy!" his dad said.

"Dapper!" his mom said.

"Black and white!" Lissa said, and everyone laughed. Bethany only smiled slightly, afraid to be too obvious about how handsome she thought he looked.

As the Carlsons opened a bottle of sparkling cider and poured a glass for everyone, Lissa's date, Teddy, arrived. Teddy was just a friend, but the two had decided to go to the dance together last week. Olivia and Lily were going solo, which plenty of other kids were also doing.

After snapping tons of pictures on the front lawn in front of the magnolia tree, which was now in full bloom, Mr. and Mrs. Carlson each loaded up their car with kids to drive to the dance.

Everyone was arriving at the same time, and it was fun to see kids all dressed up. Nate had to stand at the entrance with the other newly elected class officers to greet everyone. Once most kids had arrived, everyone gathered around the stage, where Mr. Parmalee, the student council adviser, welcomed everyone and congratulated the new officers: Nate, class president; Joseph, vice president; Michelle, treasurer; and Zoe, secretary.

Then Mr. Parmalee made an announcement that caused Bethany's stomach to lurch.

"I now invite all the four elected officials to begin their term in office with a special inaugural dance." That meant that Nate would be dancing with either Michelle or Zoe. *How could this be happening?* Bethany thought. *He's my date, and he's dancing the first dance with another girl!* She bit her lip to keep from crying.

The music started, and Joseph looked at Michelle and offered his hand, which meant that Nate would be dancing with Zoe. *Zoe is really pretty,* Bethany thought. She watched as Nate placed his hands on Zoe's waist and the two danced together. Everyone made a big circle around them and watched.

It's just one song, it's just one song, Bethany thought over and over. *It'll be over soon.* She concentrated on keeping her expression neutral, not wanting anyone to see how upset she was. She thought about all the politicians' wives throughout history and the sacrifices they had to make for their husbands' jobs. *I'm going to be supportive,* she thought, *because that's my job.*

That first dance ended quickly, and the rest of the

night was great. Bethany and Nate danced plenty, as did Lissa and Teddy. Olivia and Lily danced with guy friends, and everyone took breaks at the cookies-and-punch table.

At the end of the evening, after the Carlsons had driven them home, Nate walked Bethany to her door.

"It was a great night, right?" Nate asked Bethany.

"Totally!" Bethany said, and she meant it. She couldn't believe how upset she'd felt earlier when Nate had danced with Zoe.

Then Nate leaned over and gave her a kiss on the cheek. And Bethany felt sure this had been the best night ever.

But the good feeling didn't last long. Once in bed, trying to sleep, Bethany replayed the evening over and over. The happy memories were gradually replaced with mental images of Zoe and Nate dancing, and Bethany became convinced that Nate had really enjoyed his dance with Zoe. She imagined their conversation, which she was positive had gone something like this:

Zoe: So you're here with Bethany?

Nate: Yeah, Lissa made me ask her because she has a huge crush on me.

Zoe: That was nice of you.

Nate: I know, well, what can I say, I'm a nice guy. So do you want to go to the movies with me next weekend?

Zoe: Oh, Nate, I'd love to.

She finally fell asleep, fading into a haze of paranoia and heartbreak.

BEEP, BEEP, BEEEEEP! BEEP, BEEP, BEEEEEP!

A car horn was blaring at Bethany—the headlights blinding her as she opened her eyes—and she was standing in the middle of the road.

She had sleepwalked again.

Again, again, again, it happened again, she thought.

This time she'd passed Nate and Lissa's by about a block and was standing in front of a mailbox, which she leaned against after the car had passed. Her heart was throbbing in her ears, in her throat, and in her toes.

Bethany wanted her mom. Badly. She hadn't felt this way since she was little and woke up with nightmares in the middle of the night. But both of her parents were spending the night in Manhattan. She knew she could go to Aunt Mimi if she wanted to, but she didn't want to.

She wiped her sweaty palms on her pajama pants and walked home. And then didn't sleep at all.

CHAPTER 11

Bethany felt terrible in the morning. The combination of the stress from sleepwalking and the overall lack of sleep made her feel absolutely awful.

She twisted her ring around her finger, obsessing over the idea that Nate was going to break up with her and start going out with Zoe. She couldn't take her eyes off the ring.

Enough, she thought. *I have to snap myself out of this. Maybe if I take the ring off, it will take my mind off Nate.* She did, and put it in her night-table drawer. Finally she went downstairs for breakfast. Her parents were due home tonight, and she realized how much she was looking forward to seeing them. *I'll tell Mom all about the sleepwalking, and she'll know what to do,* Bethany thought.

She chose a banana to cut up into her cereal. She realized that her mood was definitely lifting. *I was being totally paranoid. Nate really likes me,* she thought. *I don't know what my problem is sometimes.*

She spent the day reading a novel and downloading photos from the night before. There were some great ones in there, including some of Nate looking happily at Bethany—aha! Photographic evidence! She even made a few scrapbook collages with her online photo program, writing funny captions and featuring each of her new friends: Lissa, Olivia, and Lily. Nate got his own page.

At four o'clock, she was due to go over to Lissa's so they could work on some homework together. She fixed her hair and put on lip gloss, and after a moment's hesitation, put the ring back on, since she knew she was going to see Nate.

But when she got to Lissa's house, Nate wasn't there. Suddenly the good feeling disappeared, and she felt the terrible heaviness again.

"Where's Nate?" Bethany asked Lissa, trying to sound nonchalant.

"I'm not sure, actually," Lissa said, just as casually. "Let me know when you're ready to start those math problems . . . they are really confusing!" As Lissa talked about math, Bethany's mind wandered.

Now that I think about it, Nate hasn't been here the last couple of times I dropped by on the weekend. Where has he been? Is he out with someone? Does Zoe live around here? Is he out with her? She could barely concentrate on her homework.

"I'm not feeling so well. I'm going to go home and rest, okay?" Bethany said suddenly to Lissa. Without waiting for a response, she began gathering up her books and papers.

"Um . . . okay, but do you need anything? Do you want me to get my mom?" Lissa could see that her friend looked shaky and pale, and she certainly looked like something was bothering her.

But Bethany just shook her head no, and not trusting herself to speak anymore, she walked quickly from the room and then ran all the way home.

When she got home, Bethany barely even noticed her parents, who had gotten back early. She ran right by them and straight into her room. Her mom was at her door in seconds.

"What's the matter, honey?" she asked, obviously concerned.

"I'm just having a bad day," Bethany said. But her voice cracked as she said it, and tears filled her eyes.

"Oh, Bethany, come here." Her mom came over and gave her a warm hug. That helped, a little. Bethany sat in comfortable silence with her mom for a few moments and then pulled herself together and managed a brave smile.

"Welcome home!" she said, laughing. Her mom smiled and hugged her again. As her mom patted her back, she wound a strand of Bethany's hair around her finger absently.

"Your hair's getting darker," she said. Seeing Bethany's horrified expression, she quickly added, "But it's still as pretty as ever. And that's a normal part of adolescence, having your hair get darker."

"But it's also losing some of its curl," Bethany said mournfully. "And it's getting harder to part on the side. All of a sudden it has a mind of its own and wants to part itself down the middle. Lissa and Olivia and Lily said it looks 1970s."

"Well, aren't the 1970s very chic again?" her mom said with a grin. Then her voice grew more serious. "Listen, honey, is there anything you want to talk about?"

Bethany suddenly didn't feel like talking to her mom

anymore. *I'll talk to her about the sleepwalking and my problems with Nate later,* she promised herself.

"Nope, everything is great. I think I'm just tired. You know how I get when I'm tired."

Her mother looked unconvinced but let the matter drop.

CHAPTER 12

The day of the history class field trip to the graveyard and historical society arrived. Nate had texted Bethany the night before:

MILADY, TOO BAD WE CAN'T JUST MEET THE CLASS AT THE GRAVEYARD. WE COULD HAVE BREAKFAST AT MY HOUSE FIRST AND JUST WAIT FOR THEM TO ARRIVE.

Bethany's heart skipped a beat. She wrote back:

I KNOW, RIGHT?

Nate wrote back:

MR. PARMALEE LOVES THIS FIELD TRIP. IT'S LEGENDARY! SEE U TOMORROW, MILADY!

Again, her heart skipped a beat. She tried to wait a few minutes before she texted back:

TILL TOMORROW, THEN, MILORD.

And now it was tomorrow. Bethany and Nate sat together on the bus on the way to the graveyard and listened to Mr. Parmalee.

"First stop is the old town graveyard, where we'll do gravestone rubbings," he said. "I know Nate and Bethany are probably familiar with it, given that they live next door, but most of you haven't had a close look. I've got the paper and charcoal here and will distribute them and do a demonstration when we arrive. You can do as many rubbings as you want, but be sure to capture the names and dates on the gravestone you're recording. The student who finds the earliest date will get a prize." He really did seem excited.

"Afterward, we'll go to the historical society, where there's something I know you're all waiting to see: a lock of Lady Warwick's hair in a glass vial."

The kids reacted to this bit of information with a combination of intrigue and disgust. Centuries-old hair!

When they arrived at the graveyard, Mr. Parmalee passed out paper and charcoal sticks. As promised, he demonstrated how to do a gravestone rubbing: You placed the paper on the gravestone, then rubbed the charcoal over the whole paper until you saw the words on the stone "appear" on the paper. He chose Lady Warwick's gravestone, which, he explained, didn't mark an actual grave but was just a memorial site, because Lord Warwick had requested that her stone be moved next to his when he was buried.

"Also, there was no body to bury," Nate added with a grin.

Mr. Parmalee smiled. "Right, Mr. Local Legend," he said. "The story goes that she wasn't in her coffin when it was dug up. And let's not forget about the scratch marks inside the coffin. But there's no historical evidence of either of those 'facts' anywhere. All we know is that Lord Warwick moved Lady Warwick's gravestone when he moved. Then when he died, he was buried here, and her gravestone was moved here. Too bad he's not here to explain, right?"

"Totally," Nate said.

Mr. Parmalee pointed out the dates and had the kids do the math. Lord Warwick had lived another forty-one years after Lady Warwick died. Since he was buried next to her stone and there was no one else buried on the other side, it was safe to conclude that he'd never remarried. Bethany listened with interest. *It's nice that he never remarried,* she thought, a warm feeling of happiness spreading over her.

The group dispersed to do their gravestone rubbings. Nate chose a grave from 1699.

"The first names on the graves are so interesting," Bethany said, coming up next to him. "Obed. Josiah. Mercy. Amos. Ephraim."

"Right?" Nate said. "And there are so many with the same last name. Pratt. Spencer. Lowell. Adams. Smith. Pretty different from our phone directory now, with plenty of Gionfriddos, Horowitzes, and McManuses. Guess things have gotten more diverse here in Old Warwick over the centuries."

Soon it was time to go. Everyone rolled up their

rubbings carefully and got back on the bus to go to the historical society. Mr. Parmalee sat in front of Nate and Bethany on the way.

"Bethany, did you know that Lawrence Reiney, the last president of the Old Warwick Historical Society, used to live in your house?" he asked Bethany.

"Yes, I heard that," she said.

"He was a wonderful man," Mr. Parmalee said. Bethany nodded respectfully as the bus pulled up to an old colonial home with a plaque on it: BUILT IN 1710.

"Math quiz!" Mr. Parmalee called out to the class. "How old is this building?"

Everyone did the math in their heads. Everyone except Bethany, who couldn't concentrate when she was sitting this close to Nate.

But she liked the exhibit inside. Besides the vial with a lock of Lady Warwick's straight black hair inside, which was a big hit with the group, it turned out that the exhibit had a lot to do with Bethany's research topic of women's role in colonial Old Warwick.

There was a lot of framed embroidery that Bethany learned were called samplers. Women were supposed to show off their sewing skills to potential husbands, and the sampler was like their portfolio. Bethany was glad she didn't have to do a sampler for Nate, or knit any of the handmade lace that was on display. *I don't think I'd be very good at that,* she worried silently.

CHAPTER 13

The last day of school finally arrived. Lissa had announced that it was the perfect occasion for a sleepover. She, Olivia, and Lily had celebrated the end of the school year last year with a last-day-of-school sleepover too, so this would be the second annual one. The girls, excited that it was almost time to initiate Bethany to the Sandy Lady club, were thrilled to add yet another tradition to their roster. But that morning Bethany texted Lissa to say she was staying home from school and wouldn't be able to come to the sleepover because she wasn't feeling well.

"What's wrong, honey?" Bethany's dad asked as he stuck his head into her room first thing in the morning. She should have been getting dressed for the last day of school, but she lay in bed, eyes open, staring at the ceiling.

"I really don't know where to begin," Bethany said slowly and softly. Her dad looked concerned. "I just feel bad everywhere," she added.

Her dad came over and felt her forehead. "You don't seem to have a fever. I wish your mom was still here, but she's left for work already. Maybe you ought to stay home. Do you really want to miss the last day of school, though?"

"I think I have to," she said.

"Okay, then," her dad said. "Go back to sleep. You haven't been sleeping very well lately, have you?"

"No," Bethany admitted. She tried not to start crying.

"Well, Aunt Mimi will be here in case of an emergency. But call Mom or me at work around lunchtime and let us know how you're doing, okay?"

"Okay," Bethany whispered, closing her eyes. She really did feel horrible, though it wasn't anything she could put her finger on, like a sore throat. It was just all-over horrible.

She fell back asleep and woke up at noon feeling exactly the same way. She reached for her cell phone and called her mom at work.

"Hi, Mom," she said. She was surprised at how weak her voice sounded.

“Bethany, you sound terrible,” her mom said kindly. “Do you feel as bad as you sound?”

“Yes,” Bethany said. “I don’t know what’s the matter with me.”

“Can Aunt Mimi make you some lunch?”

“I don’t think so,” Bethany said. Everything was so sad. Now she couldn’t stop the tears from coming, and she sobbed into the phone.

“I’m so sorry you feel so bad,” her mom said. “I’m going to come home from work and take you to the doctor.”

Even though Bethany felt awful, she remembered to take her ring off before going to the doctor. Her mom still hadn’t said anything about it, and Bethany wasn’t sure if her mother had even seen her wearing it. She didn’t want to run the risk of having the doctor ask her about it.

Bethany had never been to this doctor before, having moved to town so recently. Dr. Coppola was a nice guy, giving her a full checkup and asking lots of questions. Her mom sat in the room during the exam.

Finally Dr. Coppola took off his stethoscope and said, "Has anything been bothering you lately, Bethany? Are you stressed out in your new school, anything like that? Are you making new friends here in town?"

"Um, no," she mumbled. "I mean yes, I'm making friends, and no, I'm not stressed out." The doctor raised his eyebrows, and Bethany realized he thought she was faking being sick.

"She's awfully pale, isn't she, Doctor?" Bethany's mom asked. Bethany was pleased that her mom was sticking up for her.

"Probably nothing a little fresh air can't fix." Dr. Coppola smiled at both of them. "I can't find anything wrong with her. But call me if she starts running a fever."

In the car on the way home, Bethany's mom said, "You've been upset about Nate, haven't you, honey?"

Bethany felt trapped. Her mom always did this: started serious conversations in the car when she knew her daughter couldn't escape.

"Did something happen at the dance? Something that's been bothering you?" her mom continued.

"No, Mom." Bethany tried to keep her voice level. The truth was, she felt like she was going crazy, and if she started talking, her mother would know how crazy she was, and might even suggest she not see Nate anymore if he was upsetting her so much.

Now would be a good time to mention the sleepwalking, Bethany thought. "There is one thing," she said slowly, and her mom raised her eyebrows and nodded for her to continue.

"Something really weird has been happening. It's happened twice." Bethany took a deep breath and continued. "I've been sleepwalking," she said.

Her mom smiled gently. "That used to happen to me when I was your age too," she said.

"Really?" Bethany said, flooded with relief.

"Yes. My parents took me to the doctor, and he said it was normal and I'd grow out of it. And I did. It can be scary, but you'll grow out of it too. Did this happen while Dad and I were out of town?"

Bethany nodded, and her mom looked at her with so much love and concern that Bethany wished she had told her weeks ago. "I'm so sorry. You must have been so scared! You didn't fall down or anything, did you?"

"No, nothing like that," Bethany assured her mom. *She thinks I just walked around the house. I am definitely not telling her I woke up down the street!*

She suddenly felt better than she had all day. When they got home, she accepted a Popsicle from her mom and went straight back to bed, where she slept till dinnertime. She heard her parents eating downstairs and went down to join them.

"There she is," her dad said, putting his fork and knife down. "Let me feel your forehead." The back of his hand felt cool on her face. "You're not warm," he said, relieved.

"Honey, maybe Dr. Coppola's idea about fresh air is a good one," her mom said. "Why don't you get dressed and take a little walk?"

"You're going to insist on this, aren't you?" Bethany sighed.

"I'm afraid so." Her mom nodded. "Too much time in bed is bad for your mood."

"Okay, maybe you're right," Bethany said. Her parents seemed surprised and delighted by her new attitude. She went upstairs and put on comfy shorts and a T-shirt. And then she realized her finger was still bare, and she put her beloved ring back on.

As she walked down her front path, Bethany had to admit it was a beautiful evening. Maybe her parents and Dr. Coppola were right. Maybe all she needed was some fresh air. She twirled the ring on her finger and breathed deeply. *He wouldn't have given me this ring if he didn't really like me,* she told herself as she started down the sidewalk to the Carlsons' house, which had a huge porch that spanned the front and sides of the house. A wraparound porch, her mother called it.

The Carlsons' place was all lit up from the inside, and Bethany had a great view from the sidewalk. It looked so cozy in there. First she noticed Lissa and Lily at the dining room table. They were eating, maybe, or playing a board game or something. And on the side porch . . .

On the side porch . . . on the side porch . . .

Bethany swallowed hard.

On the side porch stood Nate and Olivia, talking to each other. Nate was moving his hands and arms in a very animated way, and Olivia looked like she was laughing.

Bethany felt light-headed. What was going on between the two of them? Was *Olivia* Nate's new girlfriend? She ran home, got back into bed, and cried herself to sleep.

Well, it turned out the fresh air certainly hadn't helped.

CHAPTER 14

As Bethany was sobbing herself to sleep, Lissa, Olivia, and Lily lay in the dark in their sleeping bags.

Soon they would be eighth graders! *Life is good,* Lissa thought as she listened to her friends chat softly. The only bummer was that Bethany couldn't be there, and they didn't really understand why. What exactly was she sick with? Her text message had been so vague: SICK AT HOME, SORRY WILL MISS SLEEPOVER . . .

They had texted back: WHAT'S THE MATTER? But she had not responded.

"Seriously," Lily was saying. "She's been acting even stranger lately."

Olivia snorted. "It's because she's in *love*!" she crowed, a touch of disdain in her voice.

"No, really," Lily said. "It seems like more than that. She used to be so energetic and happy, and now she's all dark and gloomy. And she seems so insecure about Nate. She wasn't like that when we first met her. Remember our first sleepover, when she talked about her last boyfriend, she was all, like 'whatever' about him?"

"That's true," Lissa chimed in. "Nate said something to me about it, actually."

"He *did*?" Lily and Olivia said at the same time.

"Yeah," Lissa said, feeling slightly guilty for betraying her brother's confidence. Not so guilty, though, that she didn't continue. "He said she's been acting really weird. Which is funny coming from him. He's basically the weirdest person I know!" Lily and Olivia laughed, and Lissa went on.

"He said she's been acting really jealous, like she thinks he's going to start going out with someone else, even when he's with his guy friends. Like even when he goes fishing off the pier, she gets really mad at him. How bizarre is that?"

Olivia sighed. "That's so silly. He totally likes her, and she's so pretty and smart and funny. She has no reason to think he's not into her anymore."

"I agree," Lissa said. "But he says she's totally serious about thinking he likes someone else. That and him going fishing off the pier make her get all crazy with him."

"Maybe she thinks he'll fall in and get eaten by the fish," Olivia said, and they all cackled with laughter at the thought. Then there was a long silence.

"Kidding aside . . . are you guys thinking what I'm thinking?" Lily asked mysteriously.

"It depends," Olivia said. "What are you thinking?"

"I know it's a mad crazy theory, but have you noticed that the way she's changing totally matches Lady Warwick?" Lily said.

Lissa and Olivia began howling with laughter, which Lily did not appreciate. She waited patiently for her friends to stop laughing.

"Okay, Miss Ghost Story, do tell us your mad crazy theory," Lissa said, which sent them all into peals of laughter again. This time Lily joined in. But then she got herself together and spoke while Lissa and Olivia were still gasping for breath.

"You really wanna know? Okay, doubters," Lily said in a serious tone. "First, she *looks* like Lady Warwick. Her hair is darker and less curly, and it's parted in the middle now."

Lissa and Olivia stopped laughing. That was true.

"Second, she's *acting* just like Lady Warwick did with Lord Warwick, all convinced he's having an affair, and all mad that he's going fishing with his friends."

"I'm so sick of all this talk about fishing!" Olivia interrupted her. "What does the fishing have to do with it?"

"Haven't you read the story framed by the stairs here?" Lily asked her. "Lady Warwick didn't like Lord Warwick going on long fishing voyages. She worried when he was out at sea."

"Sometimes I wish Nate *would* go out to sea for a while," Lissa said, trying to get everyone laughing again and off this creepy topic, but the others were silent.

Lily continued. "And the story says she was beautiful and intense. Well, we know Bethany's beautiful. And when we met her, she seemed totally normal. But now I think the best word to describe her is definitely *in . . . tense*," she said slowly, drawing out the word.

And then, as if on cue, they heard it.

The wind rattling the window. *Scratch, scratch, scratch. Tap, tap, tap.*

"It's her! It's Lady Warwick!" Lily cried, and all three girls screamed in terror.

CHAPTER 15

Mr. Carlson came running in, looking half-alarmed and half-annoyed.

"What's going on?" he asked, a little out of breath from his sprint.

"We heard tapping at the window," Lissa said, still feeling the fear move through her whole body. "I'm sure it was Nate trying to scare us," she added quickly. She hadn't used that "tattling" tone on her brother in a while and felt sort of immature for doing so now. Still, it was the only thing that could explain what they'd heard.

"You think so, huh?" her dad said. "I'm pretty sure he's in bed reading. Well, let's get him in here and find out." He turned and left the room.

"It had to have been him," Lissa told her friends,

who had calmed down a little but were still out of breath from screaming so loud and hard. Soon Mr. Carlson returned with a sleepy Nate, who was shuffling behind him and looking very grumpy.

"I was half-asleep," he snapped groggily. "Thanks a lot for blaming me for being total scaredy-cats," he added.

"Nate, I'm sorry we got you up, but we had to be sure it wasn't you," Mr. Carlson said.

"Why don't you all go wander around in the graveyard together and search for Lady Warwick's ghost, since you seem so convinced it was her," Nate said with true disdain. "And since you're such scaredies, you can hold hands out there in a row to protect yourself from the big spooky ghost."

"That's enough, Nate. It wasn't too long ago you got spooked by little noises in the night too. You can go back to bed now," Mr. Carlson said.

Bethany wasn't sleeping well that night either. She kept dreaming she was lost in the woods by herself. Then she'd wake up and hope the dream wouldn't continue. But it always did.

A loud tapping sound woke her up, and sure enough, she was standing up in some sort of field in her pajamas.

Another sleepwalking incident.

Bethany looked at her own hand and saw that she herself was using the ring to make the tapping sound on some sort of metal plaque that was affixed to a large rock in the middle of a small field.

The plaque read LORD ELIJAH WARWICK AND LADY ALICE WARWICK, FOUNDERS OF OLD WARWICK SETTLEMENT, LIVED HERE 1659–1662.

Now she knew where she was. She remembered Mr. Parmalee saying that Lord and Lady Warwick's original home was just a few blocks from the graveyard. It was the site of Lord Warwick's home that he had burned to the ground after burying Lady Warwick alive. She hadn't walked too far. It was just a few blocks past Nate and Lissa's house, but she hadn't been there before. What was she doing there now?

Bethany walked home, crept inside silently without waking her parents, and got back in bed. She took off the ring and put it on her night table. Then she slept a dreamless sleep.

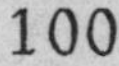

In the morning Lissa, Lily, and Olivia were all mortified by their screaming the night before. They could barely look at Nate as they sheepishly ate their waffles.

Lissa's parents didn't say anything about it. But Nate spoke right up.

"In the interest of full disclosure, I have something to tell you all," he said. Sometimes he sounded like a real politician, Lissa thought. Everyone looked at him.

"It obviously wasn't me last night, but it *was* me that first time, when Bethany was here," he said. He seemed proud of himself for his honesty.

"You mean Bethany's first sleepover?" Lissa asked.

"Yes." Nate looked like he couldn't figure out whether to grin proudly or duck his head sheepishly. He was doing a bit of both.

"I was out there with a branch," he confessed. "And once I heard how loud you were all screaming, I stopped."

"Okay, Nate." Mr. Carlson sighed. "Your honesty lessens your punishment. Of course, you are still punished. Your morning is going to consist of weeding the garden with your parents."

Nate headed outside with his parents, and Lissa turned to her friends. "I feel really badly for talking about

Bethany last night," she said quietly. Remembering their first sleepover had reminded Lissa of how close they had all grown since then.

"Me too," said Olivia. And Lily nodded in agreement.

"I'm not sure what's going on with her, but we wouldn't be good friends if we didn't try to help her. I was thinking . . . maybe we can have a do-over sleepover tonight, if she's feeling better. But before that, we can do Sandy Lady this afternoon. Really kick the summer off right!"

"Awesome idea!" Lily said.

"I'm in, of course!" Olivia added.

Feeling better, Lissa texted Bethany to ask how she was feeling and to find out if she could do Sandy Lady later that day, and then come over for a do-over sleepover.

Bethany woke to the sound of Lissa's text coming in. She read it and smiled.

Getting out of bed, she pulled on her favorite green summer tank top, which was the exact color of beach glass, and her favorite jeans shorts. Seeing her ring sitting on her nightstand, she picked it up and put it on her finger. *It's time to tell Mom and Dad that Nate is my boyfriend,* she thought happily.

Then she went downstairs with a slight spring in her step. She poured herself a big bowl of granola and sat with her parents and Aunt Mimi as they finished their coffee.

"It's nice to see you eating bigger portions," her mom said. "You've been eating like a bird lately."

"I think I'm all better," Bethany said, pouring milk to cover the granola. There was a bowl of blueberries on the table, and she added a big scoop of those, too.

"Good thing," her dad said. "Just in time for the first real day of the summer. The Carlsons have invited us to go antiquing with them today. Will you be hanging out with Nate and Lissa today?"

Bethany smiled around her spoon. "Yes, Lissa just texted me about coming over. Oh, and Lissa, Lily, and Olivia are going to initiate me into their Sandy Lady Club."

"Do tell," her mom said.

"They bury each other in sand," Bethany explained. "They dig a big hole and take turns completely burying each other. Except their heads, of course. They do it at the beginning of every summer, to mark the start of the season."

"Sounds fun," her mom said. "You'll need a good shower afterward."

"I know," Bethany said happily. "Lissa, Olivia, and Lily have been doing it every summer since fifth grade, and this year they're including me."

"You know, I'm so proud of you for making the best of this move," her dad said. "We thought it would be so hard to move in the middle of the school year, but you've made such good friends."

Her mom grinned. "And even a *special* friend," she added slyly. "Did he give you that ring you've been wearing?"

So much for me thinking Mom wouldn't notice it, Bethany thought. But as she looked at her mom's smiling face, she realized her mom didn't seem to mind.

"He did give it to me," she confirmed.

"It looks expensive," her dad said, leaning over the table for a better look. Bethany quickly pulled her hand away.

"Oh, I'm sure it's just costume!" her mother said. "I can't imagine the Carlsons would allow him to give her something *real*!"

Bethany kept her head down and smiled a secret smile as she looked at her beloved ring.

CHAPTER 16

But by the time she'd packed her bag for the beach and the sleepover, Bethany's mood had begun to plummet. She felt the sickness start creeping through her body, though she didn't say anything to her parents about it. She was starting to realize that maybe it was in her head, after all. Maybe she was nervous about seeing Nate? She had been so excited that same morning, but now she was filled with dread. *Why do I keep feeling like this?* she thought. *Enough with the dread!*

She headed over to Lissa and Nate's, trying hard to ignore the sinking feeling inside. But by the time she arrived, the paranoid, depressed feeling she'd had when she was so sick yesterday had returned. Just in time for Nate to open the door.

"Hello, milady," he said with a smile. "Glad you're feeling better."

If you only knew, Bethany thought. Before she could stop herself, she said coldly, "Why didn't you come see me when I was sick?" She hadn't even realized she was so upset about this until she said it.

"Um, actually, I did," Nate said, looking a little hurt. "I brought you a scone. Your parents said you were asleep. Didn't they tell you? Didn't they give you the scone?"

"No, they didn't," Bethany shot back. "Where were you, anyway? Off on a fishing voyage?" She sounded so angry that she barely recognized her own voice.

"What?" Nate said, confused. "You know what? You're acting a little weird."

Here it comes, thought Bethany. *He's going to tell me he's met someone else.*

"I'm sorry," she said quickly. "I haven't been sleeping too well." Couldn't she just hit the reverse button and make this conversation go differently?

Nate was staring at the ground, so Bethany continued. "I've been sleepwalking, and it's really freaking me out," she said. "Last night I wound up at the old Warwick house with the plaque. I don't know how I got there."

"Really?" Nate looked right at her. Well, she certainly had his attention now. "That's *really* weird," he said. "Sorry that happened to you." But then something in Nate seemed to shift.

"It's just kind of frustrating," he went on, looking down again. "You used to be different. Now it just seems like you're mad at me all the time. You're acting kind of crazy."

Bethany thought she couldn't feel any worse than she had yesterday, but she suddenly reached a new low. *That's it, he's breaking up with me,* she thought over and over as she twirled the ring. *He's going to ask for the ring back, I just know it.*

"Do you want the ring back?" she asked softly. She could hear her heart beating in her ears.

"No, milady, I certainly don't," Nate said. He sounded pretty sure of himself, but Bethany was still wild with fear inside.

"I just want you to stop acting so weird," he added. "You have no reason to be acting like this."

He likes someone else, Bethany thought. *Someone who doesn't act so strange. He says he doesn't want the ring back, but*

I'm sure he doesn't want to be with me anymore. Before she could stop herself, she blurted, "Just leave and go on a fishing voyage like you always do!"

Nate gave her a long, hard, look. "Are you for real, Bethany?" he blurted out in anger.

She stared back at him in stunned silence.

But then he seemed to gain control over his emotions. He took a deep breath and in a much calmer voice said, "Actually, I did plan to go fishing with my friends today. Not on a voyage. Just to the pier, with Justin and Russ. Your friends are upstairs waiting for you." And with that, he walked away, leaving the front door open for her to come in and meet up with Lissa, Lily, and Olivia.

Bethany stood there for a minute before entering, trying to recover from the horrible exchange. She wanted to pull herself together before seeing her friends. She didn't want them to think she was crazy too, like Nate obviously did. Then she would have no boyfriend *and* no friends. She really had to watch it. *The ring is still on my finger,* she tried to reassure herself. *Which means we're still officially together.*

"It really is cool having your backyard be a beach," Olivia was saying to Lissa as they walked onto the sand. They stopped near the crooked tree, which, Lissa explained to Bethany, was hundreds of years old and was always the site of the Sandy Lady ritual.

"Cool!" Bethany said, trying to act normally. She thought she'd done a pretty good job so far with her friends, who didn't seem to notice anything was wrong.

Then suddenly Lily said something to Bethany that made her freeze inside. "Look at me," she said in a serious voice.

Bethany looked at Lily, forcing herself to meet her friend's eyes. Lily looked hard back at Bethany, staring into her eyes for what seemed like an eternity. *She's going to tell me I'm crazy,* Bethany thought.

"Your eyes look totally green," Lily said.

"What?" Bethany said. Now all three girls were examining Bethany's eyes.

"It's true," Lissa said. "Your eyes are bright green! Maybe it's the green shirt."

"Or the new summer sun!" Olivia said happily, oblivious to the fact that Bethany was feeling just the opposite of sunny.

"My eyes change color a little depending on the light and what I'm wearing," Lissa said. "That's probably what it is. They look really pretty. They match your shirt perfectly."

Okay, so my eyes look green, Bethany thought. *If that's the worst of what they notice about me, that's pretty good.*

"Sandy Lady! Sandy Lady!" Lissa, Lily, and Olivia cried. It was time to begin the summer ritual.

"How do you decide who goes first?" Bethany asked, trying to feign interest in the ritual, despite the fact that she had a strong feeling of dread growing in her chest.

"Well, last time when it was the three of us, we did eeny-meeny-miney-mo," Lissa said. "But this time, since it's a new year and there's a new member of the club, I think we should do something different. Like rock, scissors, paper."

"Totally," Lily and Olivia said at the same time.

The rock, scissors, paper routine turned out to be complicated, and it took awhile to work out the logistics. Finally they got it right.

"I'm the first Sandy Lady of the summer!" Lissa crowed as they all dug a long hole in which she would be buried. It took awhile, because they were using their hands and because they wanted to make it as deep as possible. Then Lissa took off her shorts and top to reveal her new polka-dot bathing suit. She got in and lay down faceup as the other three threw sand on her until all they could see was her head.

They patted the sand down on top of her body, even sitting on it, so it was as tightly packed as possible. Then they all stood back to admire their work and take pictures with their phones. Lissa seemed to enjoy being buried and begged the others to bury Olivia right next to her, but Lily insisted that Sandy Lady was a one-at-a-time deal. They couldn't mess with tradition, she said, or the ritual would lose its magic and they wouldn't have a good summer.

Lissa stayed buried for about ten minutes before she asked to be dug out, and it took a few minutes to unearth her and a few hands to pull her up. She was caked in damp sand but seemed invigorated. Olivia was already getting herself ready, handing her phone over to Bethany.

"Will you document my Sandy Lady moment?" she asked Bethany.

"No problem," said Bethany. She was feeling a little better by now; things seemed to be going fine, and she was able to go along with the fun. *See, this isn't so bad!* she thought. But for some reason she was dreading her turn.

She dutifully snapped away with the phone once Olivia was buried. Olivia was making funny faces the whole time.

"Build me a mermaid tail!" she said. "Please?"

The girls went to work piling more sand on the area below Olivia's buried feet, shaping it into a curly sort of fin. Lissa used a stick to draw scales like a real mermaid.

"I'm a Pretty Mermaid Lady!" Olivia cried. "Bethany, take more photos!" Everyone was cracking up, and Bethany tried to laugh too. But half of her was thinking about Nate and how he said she used to be different.

She sighed silently, because it was true. She'd lost what had always been her superpower: her confidence. It was just gone, or misplaced, or buried, or something. Whatever it was, it wasn't here. It had been replaced by a feeling of doom so great it felt like it was burning holes in her heart. But she smiled as everyone helped Olivia out of her mermaid hole.

Now Bethany and Lily had to do rock, scissors, paper to determine who would be buried next. Bethany did "scissors" and Lily did "rock." *Yes!* thought Bethany. *Rock smashes scissors. I don't have to go next.*

So it was Lily's turn. Lily wanted the girls to build a pyramid of sand on top of her so she could pretend to be a mummified Cleopatra in her underground tomb, which kind of creeped Bethany out. But again, she went along with the sand play, helping build the pyramid and taking photos all the while.

"Sandy Cleopatra Lady, Sandy Cleopatra Lady!" Lily chanted in a singsong voice. Then, again, everyone helped her out of the hole. Bethany was beginning to feel really nervous.

Then it was her turn.

"You know what, you guys?" Bethany said nonchalantly. "I think I'll skip Sandy Lady. Maybe I'll wait till next year." The girls looked at her as if she had said she never wanted to eat cookie dough again.

"What are you talking about?" Lissa said.

"I-I-I don't know . . . ," Bethany stammered, still trying to sound like it was no big deal. "It's just, well, I just got over being sick and all. Maybe all that dampness isn't such a good idea."

"But you're fine now," Lissa countered.

"But I was really sick," Bethany reminded them.

"But you seem totally better," Olivia said.

"Well, I'm better, but I wouldn't want to have a relapse." Bethany continued to try to get out of it. She just didn't want to go into that hole. Every cell of her body was screaming in protest.

"You won't have a relapse," Lily said. Well, that made three against one. Should Bethany just refuse? No, that would be too odd. And they might tell Nate that she was acting strangely with them, too.

Thinking of Nate, she lay down in the hole.

CHAPTER 17

The sand was damp and chilly. There were more rocks under the sand than there were on top of it, and the sand got coarser the deeper it was. But there she lay, and there her friends piled sand on her. It felt clammy on her body, and the burying part seemed to take forever. How many handfuls of sand did they have to put on her, anyway? It felt like a thousand. She felt the weight of the sand increase with each scoop they added, and felt increasingly claustrophobic lying there.

She reminded herself to breathe deeply. But even that was hard, with the weight of the sand on her chest. She breathed in through her nose and out through her mouth, the way her mom did when she did yoga. She even counted her breaths slowly, as her mom had taught her when she was little and needed to calm herself down. *One, two, three, four, five, six, seven, eight, nine, ten.*

It didn't help much.

"Isn't it fun, Sandy Lady?" Lissa asked Bethany.

Bethany couldn't answer.

"Do you want us to decorate you in shells?" Olivia asked her as they patted the sand down more tightly. Bethany was now completely buried. Her long hair was splayed out on the sand, but other than that, just her head showed.

Bethany tried to nod her head no, but she couldn't move.

Lily smiled at her. "You look like a mermaid with your hair out like that!" she said, as if it was a compliment. All Bethany could do was try to keep breathing and wait for it to be over.

"How do you like your first Sandy Lady?" Lissa asked her.

Bethany managed to whisper a few words.

"I . . . changed . . . my mind!" she said slowly and softly.

"What?" Lissa said.

Bethany was finding her voice a bit better now.

"Start thy digging . . . fair maidens . . . and do free me!" she whispered.

"What'd she say?" Olivia asked. The others leaned in.

"My heart be broken . . . good ladies . . . do render me free!" she whispered.

"Huh? What is she talking about?" Lissa said.

"My heart be torn in two," Bethany continued. "And I want not to be in this cold earth."

Bethany was no longer buried in warm sand. Instead she was deep in cold earth. It was all rocks and hard soil, not sand and shells. She no longer smelled the carefree scents of summer: salt air, sunscreen, and the briny whiff of seaweed. Instead she smelled the rich mustiness of packed earth. She felt grubs and earthworms wriggle against her skin, and tangled roots pressing against her limbs.

Because she was not a Sandy Lady. In fact, she was no longer Bethany.

How could she make them understand what was happening and how much she needed to be free? And why did her left ring finger feel like it was on fire? It was as if the ring was burning into her skin.

She began gasping for air. The girls stood frozen in fear, just staring at her.

She tried to wiggle herself free underground but couldn't move. Then she began feeling herself fading away, as if she were about to faint. But there was nowhere to fall, because she was already down. Everything was growing dimmer at the edges, and soon she saw nothing at all.

She could barely speak, but managed to murmur two words: "My lord . . ." Then there was no more talking. Her eyes were closed, and she stopped wiggling around.

But in her head she was screaming.

Oh my God! Where am I?

How shall I ever get out of here?

My Lord, how could you do this to me?

Help! Be it known! I'm down here! Do help me!

The girls stood transfixed, all thinking the same thought: *Lady Warwick buried alive.*

CHAPTER 18

Now Lissa was the one who could hear her heartbeat in her ears. She ran with Olivia and Lily as fast as they could back to the house. They didn't stop to put on their flip-flops, and the hot sand burned their feet. Then the grass in Lissa's yard was scratchy and full of burrs. But in the panic of the moment, the girls didn't bother to complain. Adrenaline surged through their veins as they focused on the crisis at hand.

Lissa hoped her parents would still be home, that they hadn't left yet to go antiquing with the Warrens, but at home she found only Nate, sitting at the kitchen table, calmly eating a grilled cheese sandwich. He had just gotten back from his fishing trip with his friends, but they hadn't caught anything.

When the panting trio entered, Nate looked up and put down his sandwich.

"What's the matter?" He could tell something was very wrong.

"We were playing Sandy Lady . . . ," Lissa said, her voice breaking. She felt like a little girl. She hoped Nate wouldn't be scornful of the way she was acting. Of course, that was the least of her worries, she reminded herself.

Olivia grabbed Lissa's hand and held it hard. Lissa's voice was trembling so much that Olivia continued for her.

"And we buried Bethany and she kind of freaked out, and then she stopped talking and moving. She went completely still," Olivia finished.

"Well, what happened when you dug her out?" Nate asked, raising his eyebrows.

The girls stood silent. Nate pushed his chair back loudly and broke the silence. He ran straight for the door, saying sharply, "Why didn't you dig her up right away? And why didn't one of you stay with her?"

And then he was gone, out the door, sprinting toward the backyard beach.

"Oh my God," Lissa said, breathing hard and holding back tears. "He's right. What were we thinking?"

Something about the way he ran out reminded her of how serious this situation really was. She wished she could turn back time and listen to Bethany when she was saying she didn't want to be buried. Why hadn't she listened? Why had she gotten so caught up in Sandy Lady that she hadn't heard her friend's real fear?

"We're so close to the beach," Olivia said, trying to sound reassuring to the others. "She was only alone for a minute or two."

No one moved.

"Well, come on!" Olivia said to her two friends, who seemed to be standing frozen. "Let's get back there already! Hurry!"

It was as if Lissa and Lily had been slapped. They quickly snapped out of their stupor, and the three of them ran back to the beach.

As they approached, they breathed sighs of relief when they looked for Bethany's head in the sand and didn't see it. *Thank goodness, he must have pulled Bethany out,* Lissa thought, tears springing to her eyes.

They could see Nate in the distance, standing next to where Bethany had been. But there was no sign of Bethany.

As they approached Nate, they still saw no Bethany. Just Nate looking around.

And the hole barely looked like it had been dug up. The sand was practically undisturbed, still all neatly patted down. Bethany just wasn't in the hole anymore. That was the only difference.

"She told me she took gymnastics in New York City," Olivia said weakly. "Maybe that's how she got out of the hole without messing up the sand."

Nate stood next to it, shading his eyes, looking up and down the beach for her.

"What *exactly* happened? Break it down for me," he said impatiently, as he dug furiously in the sand where Bethany should have been. He sounded a lot like their father, Lissa thought.

"We buried her in the sand, and we don't think she liked it," she said, trying not to cry. She realized with shame just how much Bethany hadn't wanted to be buried, and how uncomfortable she'd been down there. Lissa felt just terrible. Why hadn't she been more sensitive? *Bethany always seems like she can take care of herself,* she thought. *I guess I just thought she was being dramatic.*

"She was talking strange, like in a whisper, and

using really old-fashioned words like 'Start thy digging, maidens,'" Olivia added. "She said she was heartbroken. We didn't know what she was talking about."

"She said she was . . . *heartbroken*?" Nate said slowly and deliberately.

"Yes. And she said 'my lord.' That was the last thing she said before we ran home," Lissa told Nate.

"And now we don't see her anywhere," Nate said angrily. "She's obviously run off."

"But the sand hasn't been dug up," Olivia pointed out.

"But she's not here," Nate said, sounding increasingly angry.

"I see that, but like Olivia said, the sand hasn't been dug up," Lissa said, and then realized that this was no time to bicker. "Okay, let's go up and down the beach, looking for her. Two of us will go in one direction, and the other two will go in the other direction. We'll meet back here in twenty minutes. Do you guys have your phones?"

"Wait," Nate said. He didn't sound mad anymore. He sounded puzzled. He was staring intently at the sand, into the hole he had dug up.

"What?" Olivia and Lissa cried in unison.

"Her ring," he said in disbelief, pointing. It was

true. The ruby ring lay in the sand, in exactly the place Bethany's hand had been.

"Why would she have left her ring?" Lily said, speaking for the first time. "She loves that ring."

"Because she's mad at me," Nate said, feeling his own composure start to crumble now. "We sort of had a fight." His stomach hurt as he remembered the conversation at the door just a few hours ago. Had he upset her so much that she would actually run away? Where *was* she?

"I'm sure it's not your fault," Lissa said to her brother. "She's been acting like such a drama queen lately. Come on, take the ring and let's split up and look for her."

Nate bent down and put the ring on his pinky finger. It went on only halfway.

Lissa and Nate went in one direction along the shore, Olivia and Lily in the other. Both pairs passed only happy families and kids playing in the waves. Everything in the world seemed so normal.

Except this.

When they got back to the spot Bethany had been buried, they all expected to find her sitting there, laughing. "Fooled you!" But no Bethany.

They went back to the house to try to figure out what to do. In silence, they sat at the kitchen table, where Nate's unfinished grilled cheese still lay. *Everything was so normal when I started eating that,* he thought, *and now everything is so different.*

"We have to tell her parents," Lily finally said.

"We can't," Lissa snapped. "They're out antiquing with *our* parents, remember? And we can't tell her aunt. She couldn't deal with it. We were so dumb to leave Bethany alone. We'll be in huge trouble. Let's just find her, and then Bethany can tell them the whole story if she likes. But first we need to *find her*."

CHAPTER 19

Nate grabbed a paper and pencil and started sketching their search area. He quickly ruled out the beach area, which they'd already searched. Instead he tapped the pencil on the woods area of his map.

"We'll begin in the woods behind the graveyard," he said. The girls were secretly relieved that he was acting as if he were in charge. Usually Lissa would resent him being so bossy, but not this time.

"And we'll stay together," Nate said sternly. "It'll get more confusing if we split up and meet back here. And you guys will probably get scared," he said, but not meanly. The girls were relieved they'd be sticking together. In fact, they were already holding hands.

"If she's not in the woods, we'll check the beach

again," Nate continued. "She couldn't have gone far. She doesn't even have a bike or skateboard." He was acting serious, but not panicked. Lissa noticed again how much he was acting like their dad, and she was glad he was. Her dad was great in an emergency. Lissa wished her mom and dad were really there right now.

The four went out the back door straight into the woods, passing the tree house that Nate and Lissa's dad had built them so long ago, where they used to spend so much time. It had been a year or so since they'd been up there.

"The tree house!" Lissa said. "You know she's hiding in the tree house, playing a trick on us. I'm going to kill her!" Before she'd even finished her sentence, Nate was climbing the rickety ladder.

"She's not up here," he called down.

"You've got to be joking," Lissa called up as she exchanged looks with Olivia and Lily. Nate was already on his way down.

"Let's keep going into the woods," he said. They all began walking when Olivia stopped.

"I know exactly what's going on," she said confidently.

"You *do*?" Lissa and Lily said at the same time. Lissa

should have known Olivia would mastermind the situation and figure it out. Between Nate's confidence and Olivia's logic, everything was going to be okay. Lissa breathed a deep sigh of relief.

"I certainly do," Olivia said. "She's playing a trick on us. She's hiding somewhere really hard to find. She's being a total drama queen, like Lissa said, and she's trying to scare us. Or scare Nate, that is." She looked pointedly at Nate.

"What are you talking about?" Nate snapped. "This is the unfunniest practical joke there is."

"Everyone knows she'd do anything to get attention from you, Nate," Olivia said in a serious voice.

Nate sighed loudly. "Just cut it out!" he snapped. "Let's focus on finding Bethany, okay?"

"What if she doesn't want to be found?" Lily asked suddenly in a small voice.

The other three all stopped in their tracks, lost in thought for a moment.

"Yeah," Nate said simply, fingering the ring, which was still halfway on his pinky finger. He seemed truly scared and very sad, all at the same time.

"What?" Lissa asked him. She could tell how far away

his thoughts were. Maybe it was a twin thing, but she felt very close to him at that moment.

"Why'd she leave the ring?" he asked suddenly. "Why would she have left the ring in the sand?"

Everyone was silent.

"You guys seriously have no idea at all?" Nate asked the girls. "Come on."

"We really have no idea," Lissa said earnestly. Did he think they were hiding something from him, out in the woods with their friend missing and the sky getting dark?

But Nate had a look on his face that Lissa had never seen before. She thought that she knew every single one. They shared many facial expressions. But this one was brand-new, and it left her feeling cold and even more scared.

"Let's go back," Nate said simply. The way he said it, there was no arguing. Lissa, Olivia, and Lily had no idea why he wanted to go back, but they all turned around and walked quickly back to the house. Howard was there to ambush Lissa, who was first to walk in the door. She jumped.

"Thanks, Howard, for scaring the life out of me. Great timing," she muttered. Then they all sat back down at the kitchen table and stared at one another.

Nate got up and left the room.

CHAPTER 20

Nate walked into the guest area of the B and B, which he rarely did. He went into his parents' carefully maintained historical library, which contained every book imaginable about colonial life and the history of Old Warwick. He and Lissa used to call it the "bore chamber." But at the moment, he wasn't the slightest bit bored.

He reached for the book that the Old Warwick Historical Society had published for the town's recent four hundredth anniversary, a big coffee-table book with lots of old drawings, copies of historic documents, maps, and photos of the society's collection, not all of which were on the display that Nate had viewed on their field trip.

The ring, the ring, the ring, he thought. *Milady, milady, milady. Why did she leave the ring?* He turned the pages quickly until he found what he was looking for.

A drawing of Lady Warwick's ruby ring.

The same ring that was half on his pinky finger at that very moment.

The same ring that had been on Bethany's hand when she was buried, and in the sand when she had disappeared.

We were told that Lord Warwick had everything of hers burned, Nate thought. *But I guess he didn't burn her ring.*

The girls were still sitting silent at the kitchen table when Nate entered the room, holding the book. He looked as if he had seen a ghost.

"Sit down, Nate," Lissa ordered. Now she felt as if it were her turn to take care of him. He obeyed, staring at the ring and unable to meet anyone's eyes.

"Speak," Lissa said sternly. "Out with it."

"It's my fault," Nate said slowly. "I found the ring in the sand with my metal detector. I gave it to her on her birthday."

"Nate, why are you obsessing about the ring?" Lissa said, trying to be patient. Her twin brother was really scaring her.

"It's *her* ring," Nate said softly and evenly.

"Um, right, when you gave it to Bethany, it became

hers," Olivia said, as if she were talking to a small child.

"Not Bethany's," Nate said. "Lady Warwick's."

"What are you talking about?" Lissa and Lily said at the same time.

Nate opened the book and pointed to the picture, holding his pinky finger next to the sketch of the ring for comparison. The girls crowded around to get a closer look. Nate's hand trembled, and Lissa reached out to steady it. The three girls gasped as the realization hit them.

There was no doubt it was the same ring, down to the last detail.

The only sound in the room now was everyone's shallow, steady breathing.

Then Nate spoke again. "I gave her the ring and she changed," he said in a hollow voice. "That's when she started acting jealous and possessive and sad and paranoid. Just like in that story right over there." He pointed in the direction of the staircase in the other room, where the Lady Warwick story was framed.

Lissa shook her head. *No, this can't be right,* she thought. "Go get the story. Take it off the wall," she said weakly to Olivia. Olivia ran to the staircase and brought it back, reading aloud.

"'Lady Warwick was a legendary beauty, with pale skin, emerald-green eyes, and ruby-red lips. It is said that she always wore her long black hair poker straight and parted precisely in the middle . . .'"

"Her hair," Lily whimpered, tears streaming down her face.

"Her eyes were green today," Lissa whispered.

"And she was pale from being sick yesterday," Lily added.

"It wasn't just you, Nate," Lissa said, her tears now falling as well. "We gave her something on her birthday too. The red lip gloss. The red lip gloss that made her lips ruby red."

"I bet it sealed her fate," Lily cried.

Still Olivia went on. "'Lord Warwick loved the sea and would often go on very long fishing voyages,'" she read.

"She hated it when I would go to the pier with my friends," Nate said. "And today she was babbling about me going on a voyage. . . ." His voice trailed off.

Olivia continued, "'While he was at sea, she worried about him and was also convinced he had a mistress, which wasn't true. One day Lord Warwick returned from what was to be his final voyage to find Lady Warwick very ill. She was also very angry and claimed he had broken her heart by being untrue to her.'"

"Is this getting any clearer?" Nate asked in a fierce whisper.

Olivia remained calm. "Okay, there are definitely some similarities here, but we're getting carried away. Even if the ring is the same, which I agree it appears to be, Bethany's out there somewhere playing a trick on us. We'll find her. Don't worry."

But then they all heard it.

Tapping and scratching. At the window. And it wasn't stopping.

Everyone except Olivia screamed their heads off.

Lissa screamed the loudest.

"IT'S HER!" she shrieked.

Olivia spoke loudly over the screaming. "Calm down. Remember what Mr. Parmalee said. It's a legend, remember? It's meant to scare us. Your imaginations are running away with you!"

But no one could hear her over their screams.

CHAPTER 21

After they stopped screaming, the four remained sitting at the kitchen table, staring at one another. That is, the girls stared at one another. Nate stared at the ring. They had been crying as they screamed, and now their faces were hot with tears.

Only Olivia continued to remain calm. "Come on. We're going back out there to keep searching," she said with authority as she stood up.

Lissa and Lily numbly followed her lead. She was acting like a parent or a teacher, and they were grateful, just as they had been grateful when Nate took the lead earlier.

Now the three girls stood and stared at Nate, who continued to stare at the ring.

“Come on,” Olivia said to him gently. “What are you waiting for?”

“The real question is, why are you even trying to find her?” Nate said. “She's out there, for sure. But you'll never find her.”

“If she's out there, we'll find her,” Olivia said, her voice beginning to show some signs of doubt.

“She'll be out there forever,” Nate said, his tears falling onto the pages of the book. “You can wander this town all you want looking for her, but you will never find her. Bethany is Lady Warwick. Wandering brokenhearted. For all eternity.”

EPILOGUE

FIVE YEARS LATER . . .

Lissa's mom zipped up the back of Lissa's dress and spun her around to get a good look.

"My baby girl, going to her senior prom," Mrs. Carlson said, her eyes shining with tears. "I can't believe how fast time goes."

"Oh, Mom," Lissa said. "Stop getting all senti-MENTAL!" They both laughed, and then her mom went downstairs, where Mr. Carlson was sitting with Nate on the couch. Nate was not dressed for the prom, because he was not going. Lissa had begged him to go, to bring Olivia as his date, but he refused. Nate seldom left the house, except to go to school.

Lissa had another look at herself in her full-length mirror and absently applied more lipstick.

She had a look at something else, too.

Tucked into the mirror frame was a photo of Lissa, Olivia, Lily, and Bethany with their arms around one another at their seventh-grade formal dance five years ago. It was a candid photo in which Bethany's head was thrown back in laughter, as Lissa looked her way with an amused expression. Bethany was wearing that red dress of Lissa's, and her long blond curls glowed in the late afternoon sun.

Bethany, gone forever.

Lily had moved away from Warwick the following year. She still kept in touch with Lissa and Olivia, but it wasn't the same. Nothing was the same after that day.

Lissa sat down on her bed for a few minutes with her face in her hands. It was the only way to stop her hands from shaking.

Then she stood up, took a deep breath, and headed downstairs. Mrs. Carlson looked up and said, "I'll get the sparkling cider, as is our tradition."

"Let's wait till her date gets here," Mr. Carlson said.

"Lissa and Teddy are just friends, remember, dear?" Mrs. Carlson said with a wink. Mr. Carlson laughed.

"Nate, do you think Lissa and Teddy might finally

make it official and let the cat out of the bag that they've had crushes on each other for years now?" Mrs. Carlson went on, pretending not to notice that Lissa had entered the room. Lissa just rolled her eyes, used to the teasing from her mom about Teddy. She looked expectantly at Nate to see if he'd join in the fun.

But Nate just stared out the window.

Teddy arrived and told Lissa how pretty she looked.

"You kids look great together," Mrs. Carlson said as Mr. Carlson snapped away. They convinced Nate to pose for a few pictures with his twin.

Amid the clicking of the cameras, the sound at the window was unmistakable. It was a sound Nate and Lissa had heard often over the last five years, but this time it was louder and more insistent.

Scratch, scratch, scratch. Tap, tap, tap.

Nate's eyes met Lissa's. After a moment, Lissa looked away.

Five years had gone by, and they had not grown used to it. Their parents had stopped reassuring them that it was just the wind, since their reassurances never helped.

The only thing that ever helped Nate was to put his hand in his pocket and touch the ring.

I'm sorry, milady, he thought. *I'm sorry you can't be here with us tonight. I'm sorry I can't take you to the prom. Please believe me.*

Scratch, scratch, scratch. Tap, tap, tap.

Nate was so lost in thought that he barely noticed that Lissa and Teddy were already out the door. Feeling a little dazed, he followed them out to the car.

"Are you changing your mind?" Lissa asked hopefully as she stood next to the open passenger-side door. "I know Olivia would love it if you would take her. . . ." Mr. and Mrs. Carlson also shot each other an optimistic look.

"Um, no, I'm walking down to the beach," Nate murmured.

His dad gave him a concerned glance. "Want some company?"

Nate avoided his father's eyes.

"No, thanks," he mumbled. "I've got to do this alone."

Shoulders hunched, Nate ambled down to the beach.

It was getting foggy and dark, and he couldn't see so well.

The moon was full and shining brightly in the sky, but he barely noticed.

He walked to the crooked tree and turned toward the crashing waves, his sneakers covered in sand up to the laces. But he paid that no mind. A large black bird swooped near his head. He didn't pay that any mind either.

He pulled the hood of his thick sweatshirt up over his head, stood in front of the roaring waves, and spoke softly.

"I'm sorry for all the days I went off fishing with my friends, milady. I'm sorry for every day I didn't spend with you."

His voice grew louder, and he dug his hand into the pocket of his jeans to clutch the ring.

Nate continued, "I put away all your pictures, milady, and just kept this ring to remember you by. This ring that I slipped on your finger because I loved you so. But you were never the same after that."

He paused, overtaken by sobs.

Please believe me, he thought.

After a moment, he gathered himself, held the ring above his head, and hurled it into the sea.

DO NOT FEAR—
WE HAVE ANOTHER CREEPY TALE FOR YOU!

TURN THE PAGE FOR A SNEAK PEEK AT

You're invited to a

CREEPOVER™

Together Forever

PROLOGUE

"Who-whoo! Who-whooo!"

Jennifer Howard looked up. Was that an *owl*? How could it be that late already?

She kept moving, but she could feel a nervous knot growing tighter in her throat. She knew she shouldn't be out in the woods so late, all alone.

And yet she couldn't turn back. It was as if something were leading her—pulling her even—steadily down the trail, the very same one she'd hiked with her five cabin mates earlier that day. Yes, there was the fallen tree on which Sam had somehow done a whole balance beam routine. And there was the amazing giant mushroom that her twin sister, Ali, had kicked. It lay there now, bruised and broken, and for an instant made Jennifer

annoyed at her bunkmates all over again.

And then suddenly she noticed something she hadn't seen before. Right there, where the trail veered right at the stone marker, overgrown with ferns and other twisting, gnarled weeds, another path went straight. It was much narrower than the Old Stump Trail, but it was definitely a path . . . and it was clear that Jennifer's feet, at least, thought it was the trail she ought to take.

But where did it lead? The brush was so wild and dense that Jennifer could barely see where it was safe to step. Plus, whatever light was left in the sky was quickly draining away. There was nothing but eerie, ominous shadows ahead of her—and soon behind her, as well. She pulled out her compass to try to get her bearings. Her hands were trembling and she fought against her nerves to keep them still. She waited for the needle to steady and find its way north. It finally stopped and she discovered north was exactly the way that the trail led.

Hey, she thought, her mood suddenly brightening. Directly north was Camp Hiawatha, their brother camp across the lake! What if the trail was a shortcut to the boys' camp? That would be the find of the century. Wait till she told the other girls! Now she *had* to keep going, she told herself, if only to see if the trail took her there.

She picked up her pace and pushed through the branches, trying not to get too tangled in the jutting roots or dead tree limbs. At last she burst out of the woods and into a clearing. She stopped at once and looked around.

The clearing, she could see, was about the size of a softball diamond and bathed in a misty, greenish light. The only structure was a lonely-looking, small log cabin that had to have been a hundred years old. The door dangled, cockeyed, from its hinges beneath a roof that looked ready to fall in. Of the two windows that she could see, one was broken and one was roughly boarded up. Clearly, nobody had occupied it for a very long time.

And yet it somehow didn't seem empty.

Jennifer took a half step toward the cabin.

Then paused. Something didn't feel right.

Her blood felt cold all of a sudden, as if her heart had turned to ice. *I shouldn't go any further,* she told herself, backing up, and before she knew it she was running away. But wait! She slid to a halt and her head whipped around in search of the path. All she could see was a solid black wall of trees.

The trail had disappeared.

Plus, it was night now, she realized. Way too dark to see into the woods. The clearing was somehow still glowing, but all it around it there was nothing but shadows and she could only imagine what was in there, watching her. One step in the wrong direction could mean getting lost, or injured, or worse. And who knew how long it would be until someone found her. It could be too late by the time they did.

Okay. No problem, Jennifer thought, holding up her compass and trying her best to keep her head. South. That was all she needed to know.

But when she looked down, the needle was spinning. She guessed it was just her trembling hands. But no. Her hands weren't shaking any worse than before. In fact, they were still, she realized. The needle was spinning all by itself.

Anxious, she tapped the side of the compass, but that didn't seem to help. She gave it a shake and willed it to stop already and do what it needed to do. But the harder she stared at the needle, the faster and faster it turned. Jennifer listened and could even hear it making a tiny, frantic "whirr."

Now her hands were trembling. Her whole body was, in fact.

"Who-whoo."

Startled, she jumped. Then she closed her eyes and caught her breath. It was the owl from the trail.

"Whooo."

Or was it?

She slowly turned back toward the cabin, not sure if her ears were playing tricks. Could it be that the call was coming from it?

"He-hello?" she softly called. She took another step into the clearing, and this time she didn't stop. There wasn't just something in the cabin. There was someone. Maybe that someone could help her find her way out!

"Hello?" she called again as she reached the door. She listened, but there was no answer. She waited and almost knocked. But then she noticed the broken window there right beside her. What if she simply peeked in instead? She leaned over. What remained of the glass was too caked with dirt and grime to actually see through. But the jagged hole would work, she guessed. She leaned in closer and peered through.

Was it?

Yes, it was!

There was a person sitting in there with his back to her and a hooded sweatshirt pulled down low over his head. It was a boy. At least she thought so, but she wasn't completely sure. . . .

That is until he pulled the sweatshirt back and slowly turned.

His face was pale and boyishly handsome, but it was his eyes—or lack of them, really—that Jennifer saw first. Where his eyes should have been, there were laser-like beams of greenish light. They shot straight through her and she shrank back. She tried to scream but nothing came out. Her blood, her lungs, her whole body felt numb.

Run! she tried to tell herself.

But she was too terrified to move.

Finally she managed to scramble away from the window, not knowing or caring which way she went. It didn't matter to her anymore what might be lurking out in the dark woods. She needed to get out of that clearing, she knew, as fast as she possibly could. But she'd barely run ten yards when she felt a sharp tug on the back of her shirt.

She stumbled back, afraid to turn, but she could feel a laser-like burn on the back of her head.

"Don't ever come back," said a low, haunting voice in her ear.

And that's when the scream finally spilled out of her throat.

WANT MORE CREEPINESS?

Then you're in luck, because P. J. Night has some more scares for you and your friends!

Bethany's friends search everywhere for her after she disappears from the beach, but she is never found. Can YOU find these hidden words? Words can appear up, down, backward, forward, or diagonally.

BEACH	LIGHTNING	SCHOOL
BURIED	LIPGLOSS	SLEEPOVER
CEMETARY	LORD	SLEEPWALKING
CREEPOVER	NEW YORK CITY	SPAGHETTI
CURSED	PIZZA	TAPPING
DREAM	RUBY	TOMBSTONE
EMPTY	RING	TWINS
ETCHING	SANDY LADY	VOYAGE
LADY	SCARED	WARWICK
LEGEND		WIND

READY TO SOLVE?
WE DARE YOU!

S	P	A	G	H	E	T	T	I	L	A	D	Y	D	C
L	I	E	Y	R	E	V	O	P	E	E	L	S	R	E
E	Z	D	B	I	N	V	O	Y	A	G	E	E	E	M
E	Z	E	U	N	S	C	H	O	O	L	E	S	A	E
P	A	I	R	G	L	A	U	L	R	P	N	C	M	T
W	E	R	N	N	I	C	K	K	O	I	A	A	R	A
A	C	U	R	S	E	D	K	V	W	R	A	R	H	R
L	A	B	N	I	C	K	E	T	K	A	D	E	C	Y
K	R	K	C	I	W	R	A	W	A	S	I	D	A	G
I	L	O	B	H	T	O	M	B	S	T	O	N	E	N
N	E	W	Y	O	R	K	C	I	T	Y	A	N	B	I
G	G	N	I	N	T	H	G	I	L	S	D	I	O	H
B	E	M	P	T	Y	H	G	N	I	P	P	A	T	C
A	N	D	N	I	W	S	S	O	L	G	P	I	L	T
N	D	S	A	N	D	Y	L	A	D	Y	H	I	A	E

CREATE YOUR OWN SPOOKY CHARACTERS!

One of the most fun things about writing scary stories is thinking up spooky characters. And just like people, characters need NAMES! Below is a list of spooky characters P. J. Night is working on for future stories. What would you name them? Write your answers on the lines beneath the descriptions.

Character #1: An old man who lives in a small shack near a haunted lake . . . who only comes out at night . . . when the moon is full!

____

Character #2: A woman who can change her appearance at will. But no matter what she alters, she always has a small telltale mole on her cheek!

____

Character #3: This character is a girl who is totally normal . . . except lately she's having a lot of nightmares. Then one day she dreams about a book. She goes to the library to find the book she dreamed of, and instead finds a book written by someone with her very same name . . . more than fifty years ago! And the author photo looks JUST like her! The book tells the story of a girl who is totally normal . . . but then starts having a lot of nightmares. Then one day she dreams about a book. . . .

Character #4: This character found a coin on the street and picked it up thinking it might be lucky. But not long after finding it, very strange things start happening. She decides to dispose of the coin . . . but the next day, it's back in her pocket!

Characters #5 and #6: A brother and sister duo who are very mysterious indeed. Each night they go to sleep in their beds . . . but wake up every morning in a clearing in the woods behind their house!

A lifelong night owl, **P. J. NIGHT** often works furiously into the wee hours of the morning, writing down spooky tales and dreaming up new stories of the supernatural and otherworldly. Although P. J.'s whereabouts are unknown at this time, we suspect the author lives in a drafty, old mansion where the floorboards creak when no one is there and the flickering candlelight creates shadows that creep along the walls. We truly wish we could tell you more, but we've been sworn to keep P. J.'s identity a secret . . . and it's a secret we will take to our graves!